About the Author

Award-winning author Anthony Masters knows how 'to hook his reader from the first page' *Books for Keeps.*

Anthony has written extensively for young adults and is renowned for tackling serious issues through gripping stories. He also writes for adults, both fiction and non-fiction. For the Orchard Black Apple list he has written the *Ghosthunter* series, the *Dark Diaries* series and four novels: *Spinner, Wicked, The Drop* and *Day of the Dead*, which was shortlisted for the Angus Award. He lives in Sussex with his wife and has three children.

Anthony Masters also runs *Book Explosions*, children's adventure workshops that inspire adrenalin and confidence in children, so that they can do their own creative writing.

deathtrap

ANTHONY MASTERS

ORCHARD BOOKS

ORCHARD BOOKS
96 Leonard Street, London EC2A 4XD
Orchard Books Australia
32/45-51 Huntley Street, Alexandria, NSW 2015
ISBN 1 84121 910 X
First published in Great Britain in 2003
A paperback original
Text © Anthony Masters 2003
The right of Anthony Masters to be identified as the author
of this work has been asserted by him in accordance with
the Copyright, Designs and Patents Act, 1988.
A CIP catalogue record for this book is available from
the British Library.
1 3 5 7 9 10 8 6 4 2
Printed in Great Britain

Contents

For Sarah Dudman

PROLOGUE: Night Visitor

"So give them a chance," said Jon

Barron to his son Glen. "That's all I'm asking." He went back into the lodge, leaving Glen outside. "Just think about it," he called over his shoulder.

Glen didn't immediately follow his father. Instead he decided to spend some time on his own in the Canadian spring night, not to sulk or look childish, but to give himself some space.

Then he heard the snuffling sound. Where was it coming from? Having felt the need to be on his own, Glen suddenly felt apprehensive. What *was* that noise?

Then he noticed that the dustbin at the end of the long back yard was lying on its side. Much of the contents had spilt. Something was sorting through the rubbish on the ground. Something big. Glen didn't know what to do. Should he call his father, or investigate on his own? Because his father had just criticised him Glen was determined to be independent. There were deer in the forest which came right up to the edge of the village where they were staying, as well as elk. So Glen didn't feel particularly afraid now – just a little tense, and certainly curious.

Glen also knew that there were grizzlies and black bears in the forest because that was why his father had travelled to Canada. But of course the scavenger couldn't be a bear. Bears would hardly ever come near civilisation. They were rare and frightened of human beings. He comforted himself with that reassuring thought.

Quietly, Glen approached the dustbin and to his relief the scavenger backed away. It *must* be a deer, he thought. They were nervous creatures, as nervous as he had been just a few moments ago. But now Glen felt much more relaxed, which was more than the deer felt. If it was a deer.

All Glen could see was a shadow, but there was something wrong with the shape of the shadow. Maybe it's a dog, he thought, although a voice in his mind was starting to tell him the shadow was far too big to be a dog.

There was a low growl and Glen froze, his mouth dry and sweat breaking out on his forehead. He felt as if there was something crawling on his skin.

Suddenly the creature stood up on its hind legs and Glen's mind refused to focus. The sweat was running into his eyes now and he felt a weird sensation in his stomach he'd never experienced before – a kind of deadly cold chill.

He was looking at a bear. Not a huge bear, but a bear all the same. Then Glen's mind clicked back into focus and he registered the black hair and the animal's large paws in the wan moonlight.

Glen didn't wait to check out the bear any longer, whatever its size. He turned and ran back towards the lodge, sure he was being pursued and that at any moment he would be thrown to the ground and ripped to pieces.

Glen hurled himself into the welcoming light of the

kitchen to find his father brewing coffee, and the others sitting in the living room watching TV.

"There's a bear out there," he gasped. "A black bear." Suddenly he felt as if he was going to throw up. But to Glen's fury, his warning was greeted with derisive hoots of laughter.

Intruders

Next morning Glen got up

exhausted, but determined to prove to his father
that the black bear had existed – and wasn't just a
figment of his imagination.

All night, Glen had had nightmares about the bear
rooting about in the dustbin. In his dreams, Glen was
gliding towards it, his feet hardly touching the ground,
hurtling towards the black fur under which he could
see powerful muscles rippling. Then the bear swung
round towards him, jaws open, rows of sharp teeth
shining in the moonlight. He cried out, waking up

several times, wondering if he'd been heard, only to fall asleep and plunge back into the same nightmare again.

Next morning Glen felt incredibly humiliated, unable to face the others, until Dad saw the upturned dustbin and the paw prints with his own eyes.

"There – that proves I wasn't lying to you." Glen spat out the words. He felt a heady triumph when Dad gave him a mock punch on the shoulder.

"The warden will be very concerned. He told me bears haven't been near the lodge in years."

"Maybe it was hungry," suggested Glen. "Maybe it could have had me for supper."

His father looked uneasy and then burst into speech, trying not to confront Glen's aggression. "There've been a couple of fires in the forest. Nothing big yet, and the chopper put the blazes out by dumping water on the flames. But maybe the bears are unsettled. Fire is a serious threat to them."

Glen stared at his father blankly. In his mind's eye, he could see the black bear attacking his own natural enemies, Kate and Alex, knocking them down like skittles with its huge front paws and then slashing at their throats.

This grim fate, however, was only the latest in a line of punishments Glen had been mentally meting out to Dad's new friend and her smug son. It would have been bad enough having to put up with them at home, but it was somehow far worse now Dad had decided to invite Kate and Alex on his wildlife photo shoot in Canada.

"I'll go and tell the warden," said Glen's dad, interrupting Glen's reverie.

"OK."

"And I'm sorry I didn't take you seriously." He sounded hesitant, as if he was afraid Glen was going to get angry all over again.

"I felt like an idiot last night. Everyone was laughing at me."

"We didn't mean to be cruel. We were just taken by surprise, that's all – and we couldn't believe it that easily. I'm sorry."

"Kate and Alex were trying to wind me up," said Glen. "They're always trying to—"

"You know that's not true."

"Of course it's true," snapped Glen.

With a sigh his father hurried away to see the warden.

*

When he was alone, Glen took another look at the upturned dustbin and the mess the bear had made. Again he imagined the force of a possible attack by bears on Kate and Alex. He had a momentary twinge of conscience, but this was soon overwhelmed by anger.

Kate and Alex deserved to suffer. They had openly laughed at him last night. Glen was never going to allow that to happen again. Never. He saw the black bear rearing up at them in the darkness and Kate and Alex running for their lives, screaming.

"Just look at that muscle," whispered Jon Barron, and Glen nodded back. They were standing in a treehouse that served as an observation point, overlooking the river. Bears over the age of eighteen months couldn't climb trees – so up here they were relatively safe, and could take photographs. They had been waiting by this river for hours and hours. Now, at last, a grizzly was here with her cubs.

The mother bear was trying to teach her cubs to fish from the spawning channel in the creek. She had deep chocolate-brown fur which was silvery at the tips and the distinctive humped back of the grizzly. The sparkling water around her teemed with fish. The pink salmon returned here each year from the sea to breed.

The grizzly was looking around intently, scrutinising her surroundings, wary of danger. Then, when she was satisfied the cubs were safe, she decided to continue the lesson.

Glen watched them carefully. The mother bear was a natural angler, neatly grabbing at the salmon with her paw, but her cubs were far from expert. They continually dropped the slippery salmon and didn't seem to know what to do with the fish they *did* manage to catch.

"I'm going to take my pictures from here," said Jon to Glen. "We'll only scare her off if we get any nearer."

"Won't she attack, Dad?" Glen asked.

"No way. Mother grizzlies are only interested in protecting their cubs. They don't hang around. If we disturb her she'll be off – and at quite a rate too. And keep your voice down. She'll even run from the human voice, if she hears it." He turned to the others, his finger to his lips.

Glen was glad his father was talking to him and not Kate. She was Dad's new partner, also a photographer, but without the same experience of wildlife photo shoots. She was tall and blonde and her son, Alex, was as blond as his mother, also tall and good-looking, just like Glen had always wanted to be, and wasn't. Glen hated them both.

Dad had pleaded with him to give Kate and Alex a chance, but Glen had refused to co-operate. In fact, he had been goading the intruders ever since they had all flown out to Canada from the UK. So far the enemy hadn't risen to the bait and had largely ignored him, except when they had laughed at him last night. Glen couldn't help grinning. They had stopped laughing all too hurriedly when the warden confirmed that Glen had been right all the time – and that a black bear *had* been rooting through the dustbin and could have attacked him.

"OK," said Jon, making the conversation more general. "I'm going to use a different camera with a long lens to get some close-up shots of the grizzly and her cubs. If we stay up here then they shouldn't even realise we're around. But if we were on the ground, the mother grizzly *could* attack us, if she felt very threatened."

"What do people do if they're attacked?" asked

Alex. "Run for it?"

"You have to stand still," said Glen patronisingly. "Or play dead. If you don't, the bear will race you – and win! These grizzlies can run at forty miles an hour, which is more than you can." He was deliberately rude and was pleased to see his father wince. Glen wanted to create problems – and he was getting good at doing just that.

"Where did you get that from?" asked Alex, grinning at Glen in the way that got on his nerves. He could also see his father smiling sadly and guessed that he knew Alex was right in thinking that Glen had been reading his father's wildlife books, just in case there was a chance of getting one up on his rivals, the intruders.

Now they were closer to the grizzly, Glen was relieved to see there weren't any other bears there; this was the only place you might see bears together, because usually each one stuck to his or her own territory. This morning the mother bear and her cubs had the spawning channel to themselves. Provided she continued not to realise they were there, his father should get some good shots.

Jon Barron had landed one of the most important

assignments of his life. He'd been commissioned by a top magazine to shoot grizzlies up close. Glen would have been enjoying his father's company on his own if only Kate and Alex hadn't been around. Glen had been on wildlife photo shoots all over the world with his father before, and he loved being alone with him. But now he felt as if Kate and Alex were trying to take over, to squeeze him out.

"OK," said Jon. "Here goes." He began to take shot after shot of the mother grizzly teaching her cubs to fish. Kate was also taking photographs while Alex watched the cubs in fascination.

Then, quite suddenly, a young male bear appeared at the riverbank and clambered down into the spawning channel to fish for himself.

"That's not a wise move on his part," whispered Jon to Glen.

This was like old times, Glen thought. Dad just talking to me. He glanced at the others to see how they were taking it and noticed that Kate was leaning too far out of the treehouse, almost over-balancing as she photographed the bears, seemingly unaware of the danger. In fact she was as oblivious of danger as the young male bear which was now getting too near the mother grizzly's cubs. There was going to be trouble. Should he warn Kate? Glen wondered. She was definitely leaning out too far.

Alex was still gazing at the cubs and seemed to be completely unaware of the risk his mother was taking. Any moment now, thought Glen, she'll be falling out of the treehouse. He knew he should warn her, but he didn't.

Suddenly, the mother bear launched herself at the young male and Glen was amazed by the ferocity of her attack and the speed with which she moved. Seeing her coming at the last moment, the young bear turned and ran, scrambling back up the riverbank again, while the mother grizzly growled at him threateningly, thoroughly unsettled.

Glen knew he was being irresponsible. Kate was concentrating so hard on getting the perfect shot that she still wasn't thinking about what she was doing. Just let her lean a bit further out and there could be a dreadful accident. Glen imagined Kate slipping, falling, rolling, plunging into the river. The mother grizzly would be on her in seconds. Did he care? wondered

Glen. No he didn't. To hell with her – and Alex!

Kate had one knee up now, balanced on the fence of the platform, shooting away, still edging her body forwards. Finally, Glen decided he would *have* to warn her.

"Kate." But he couldn't get the words out, his voice was a whisper, and she didn't hear. "Kate. For God's sake, Kate!" His voice still wasn't loud enough, but this time Alex heard him and he turned round in alarm.

"Mum!" he shouted. "You're leaning too far out!"

But somehow Kate still didn't hear. She was too intent on her next shot, and as she edged further out from the platform she finally lost her balance, in a split second starting to fall, catching at the branch she'd been leaning on, missing, and tumbling to the ground. Struggling to stand up, Kate only fell over again.

"Keep still!" yelled Jon from the platform.

To everyone's horror, even Glen's, Kate had fallen not far from the mother grizzly.

Kate half sat on the ground, gazing with glazed eyes at the grizzly who had turned round to face her, teeth bared. This bear wasn't running away – she was standing her ground. Glen had never seen such a display of primitive anger before. In the same moment, Alex began to climb down towards his mother. But Jon shouted, "Stay where you are!"

"I've got to help her." Alex's voice broke.

"Leave the helping to Dad!" shouted Glen, deeply ashamed that he hadn't warned Kate earlier. Why hadn't he been able to bring out the words? But the mother grizzly suddenly turned away from Kate, and pushing her cubs before her began to run on all fours towards the forest.

Soon, the grizzlies had disappeared into the undergrowth. There was no sign of them at all. Nevertheless, Glen lunged forward and gripped Alex's arm to stop him doing anything stupid. He felt good, in control, making Alex do what he was told. But at the same time, Glen wondered if the grizzlies would return.

"A female will always run if she's got cubs. Kate wasn't in danger." But Jon's voice was trembling all the same.

Kate was still rigid with fear, appalled that she'd been so stupid, so careless, and Glen's guilt increased. Still Kate sat on the ground, seemingly as unable to move as Glen had been unable to speak.

"OK," said Jon. His voice was clearer and steadier. "Come back up into the treehouse, Kate. Come on now."

Kate nodded but still didn't move, almost as if she'd been paralysed by what she'd done.

"Hurry up, Kate," yelled Glen. "The grizzlies might come back."

"They won't," said Jon confidently. "She gave the mother far too much of a scare."

Numbed and humiliated, Kate remained where she was. Then, with a sudden flurry, she staggered to her feet and began to haul herself back up to the platform.

"I'm sorry," Kate sobbed as Jon held her tight in his arms.

"Don't worry," said Jon. "It could happen to anyone."

"And I've ruined the camera."

"Too bad. What's a camera, for God's sake? It's your life we care about."

That's what you think, thought Glen as he watched his father hug Kate even tighter.

"I'm going to take you back to the lodge," said Jon, his arm still round the now shivering Kate. "We'll make some plans for you guys – but Kate needs a rest. I'm going to stay with her."

He's trying to get rid of me, thought Glen. He and his father had always been very close since Glen's mother had died in childbirth. His birth. He had often felt guilty about her death, as if he had personally killed this unknown woman, the mother he still needed so badly. If it wasn't for him, she'd be alive today, by his father's side. Instead, there was this stupid woman, and her smirking son.

Back at the lodge, Kate went to bed. After he had checked that she was asleep Jon came out into the sitting room, a finger to his lips.

"We'll have to talk quietly," he said. "I think she's gone to sleep. Now, what would you two like to do for the rest of the day?"

Glen and Jon both glanced at Alex, who had hardly said anything since they'd got back to the lodge. Suddenly he seemed to be very vulnerable and to his surprise Glen felt just a little sorry for him. Then he hardened his heart against the thought.

"We'll get some kayaking in. Alex hasn't been on the water yet," Glen suggested. He was small for his age, too small for most team sports, but determined to excel at something, he had deliberately worked on his natural love of water. Now, at thirteen, he was an expert in the kayak.

"Mind you keep to the creek then. Don't go anywhere near the river or that white water. It'll be too much for Alex – for both of you," Jon added tactfully. "But anyway, there are plenty of warning signs."

"Of course we'll keep to the creek, Dad," said Glen. But he had a swift, devilish urge to set Alex an impossible challenge. Dad was right – the white water would be far too much for Alex. But that was exactly what Glen wanted. Once again he remembered Kate and Alex hooting with derisive laughter at his fear of the bear he had seen by the dustbin. So Glen knew he couldn't pass up a golden opportunity to humiliate Alex in return.

"Well mind you do," said Dad sharply. He looked at Glen almost as if he already suspected him – or so Glen felt. "I've told you how dangerous that river is."

"What about the falls?" asked Alex. "There are notices about them everywhere."

"They're miles away," said Jon. "And I know I can trust Glen. He wouldn't do anything stupid—" He gave his son a warning glance. "Let's pack up a picnic for you both, and here's a tourist map to show you exactly where you are."

As if I didn't know, Glen thought in sudden irritation. Why did Dad have to lecture him like a young kid – especially in front of Alex?

But Jon's lecture wasn't over yet.

"Remember the forest is so dry that there's a huge fire risk."

"I know all that." Glen was getting more and more annoyed.

"Just to remind you." Dad winked at Alex. Glen realised he was trying to cheer Alex up, but he really resented that wink.

"Ready for a paddle?" Glen said to Alex as soon as his father had gone out to the kitchen.

"Sure." Alex sounded vague. He looked as if he was still slightly in shock. Glen guessed that he was so deeply relieved his mother was safe he was barely registering anything else. I'm going to really wind you up, he thought, and was shocked by the violence of his hatred. He had never felt so irresponsible.

White Water

Glen took Alex to look at the creek. The water trickled along and was very tame. They walked on in silence.

Glen was tense, knowing that Alex had been deeply alarmed by his mother's fall from the treehouse. It *had* looked pretty bad when she had slipped off, but why hadn't he, Glen, warned her earlier? If he had done, Kate would never have fallen. She could easily have been badly hurt.

Glen decided to forget about Kate. Who cared? She was all right. He knew he still wanted to humiliate Alex, though. And he was gradually forming a plan. Already he had caught a glimpse of scattered rocks and surging water. But the rapids were quite shallow here. Glen wanted something more challenging – something that was going to be too hard for a beginner – a beginner like Alex.

There were various warning notices stating *DANGER AHEAD*, but when Alex asked why they were walking past them Glen said, "Don't worry. I sussed it all out yesterday."

Alex nodded. For all he knew, Glen could have gone out to look at the river – although he hadn't.

Glen's jealousy suddenly overwhelmed all remnants of logical thought. There was Dad, probably snuggling up with Kate. Here was Alex, what a creep. But he could be taken down a peg or two. It was simple, really.

"The creek's pretty sluggish. Let's go and check the river out," said Glen. "See what the conditions there are like."

Alex nodded obediently, and they jogged all the way up the left-hand side of the creek, past the fork on the other side where the right-hand section of the creek later became the salmons' spawning channel.

Eventually the creek they had been jogging alongside joined the river and soon they came to a section where it surged down the valley, the turbulent water shallow over vicious-looking rocks. More white water, but much fiercer. Glen looked at it appreciatively. He had had a good deal of experience in these conditions and was quite confident that he could take his kayak through unscathed.

Alex was standing beside him, gazing down at the chaos. Then he turned back to Glen and their eyes met.

Is Alex trying to challenge me? wondered Glen in sudden anxiety. But how could he? Alex had never been kayaking before. Or had he? Glen was suddenly suspicious. It was that suspicion which finally made him decide to take a big risk. If Alex had been in a kayak before he might be able to beat him in calmer conditions, but you had to be a real expert to handle white water. With a bit of luck Alex would immediately capsize and he, Glen, would rescue him.

After all, the river looked shallow, no deeper than the creek. There was little danger. But there was humiliation for Alex and that's what Glen wanted. Glancing downstream he saw chains and warning notices. But they were some distance away.

Suddenly Glen felt a surge of guilt. Why was he being so rotten to Alex? Even if he *could* kayak, and for some reason hadn't told Glen, why did that really matter so much? Wasn't there a small chance they might become friends? Then Glen thought of his father and Kate cuddling up together and his heart hardened again.

"How about it then?" asked Glen.

"How about what?"

"Going in at the deep end."

"I don't get you." Was Alex stalling? Was he afraid? Glen hoped he was.

"Suppose we have a crash course on white water."

Alex shrugged, giving nothing away. "Why not?" he replied. "It looks fun out there."

"I'll give you a few pointers on land first," Glen promised as they began to retrace their steps away from the river and back to the lodge's garage where their rented kayaks were stored.

"Only one thing," began Alex hesitantly.

"What's that?" asked Glen impatiently.

"Your dad said we should only paddle in the creek

and not go near the white water – the really heavy stuff." He paused apologetically. "We shouldn't disobey him."

This is my chance, thought Glen. I can back off. He knew he should, because although the rapids looked shallow, the protective chains were there for a reason. Why *not* back off? There would be no shame in it. But Glen's hatred for Alex drove him on.

"Oh that." Glen laughed too easily. "Dad's just upset about what happened to your mum. He knows what fun the white water can be. He'll probably want to have a paddle himself later on."

"OK. Let's give it a go." Alex seemed only partly satisfied with his explanation, but he still didn't look particularly alarmed.

Glen knew that the river ran through a forest from looking at the tourist map. The details were a bit sketchy, but they showed the depth of the forest. When he had first seen the trees shaded in on a map, Glen had been amazed by the vast area they covered. As a young child, he had often dreamt of being lost in just such a deep, dark forest. It was inhabited by a gang of backwoods men who had kidnapped his mother and were holding her prisoner. The dream was childish, but Glen often remembered the dream forest and the smell of pine needles – a smell that he still found strangely menacing.

Fleetingly, as he and Alex jogged back to the lodge, Glen wondered how big the falls much further down river actually were. But then he pushed the thought away. They weren't going that far anyway.

Once at the lodge, Glen led the way round to the garage to find the kayaks, paddles, helmets, life jackets and spray decks, which are worn by the person in the kayak like a skirt – and then secured over the cockpit to stop water coming in.

Glen looked at his watch. It was after eleven. "We'll just paddle for a couple of hours or so," he said, seizing one of the kayaks by the prow and double-checking the life jacket, map, matches and the other equipment. He did the same with the other kayak.

It was the middle of June and the summer heat was already making them both sweat. Or was the sweating due to his feelings of anxiety? wondered Glen.

"Hang on!" Kate was hurrying round to the garage with what seemed like an awful lot of plastic containers. "I've made you up a picnic," she said briskly, with a return to her old confidence, although she still looked pale.

"You ought to be resting, Mum," said Alex protectively.

"I will in a minute," she replied brightly. "But I wanted to make sure you two had adequate provisions. Kayaking's hungry work." She began to pass out the plastic containers, dividing them equally between Alex and Glen who put them in their rucksacks. "Mind you stop and actually eat the picnic," she said.

Kate's like a mother hen, thought Glen. I could do without all this from her. She's not *my* mother. He looked back at the deep forest behind the lodge. Could his own mother be lost out there somewhere? Living amongst the darkness of the trees? Glen struggled to get a grip on himself. He knew his mother had died in childbirth. Why did he still have these stupid thoughts?

"Let's go." Glen felt a spurt of adrenalin as he began to drag his kayak down to the water. He would give Alex some basic instructions while they were in the creek, and then they would paddle into the river where he reckoned that Alex would soon be sorely put to the test. "OK," said Glen as Kate slipped away back towards the lodge. "To get in your kayak, you shove your paddle across the back of the cockpit and sit on it. That way you can ease both your legs forward and then slip down into the seat."

"Like this?" asked Alex.

"That's cool – but be careful," Glen warned him. He needn't have bothered, for Alex performed the task easily and within a few seconds was sitting in his kayak, legs stretched out under the prow. They were wearing tracksuit bottoms, trainers, sweatshirts and life jackets. Both wore rucksacks. Glen had shoved the tourist map and a box of matches in his and felt well prepared. He wondered how Alex felt.

Each carrying a kayak, Glen and Alex staggered down to the creek. The kayaks were light, but what with the paddles, full rucksacks and spray decks, the loads seemed to get heavier as they went. Glen was sure that Alex was as relieved as he was when they eventually reached the bank of the creek.

Glen launched his own kayak and gave a demonstration of paddling techniques. Then he showed Alex how to deal with the situation if he capsized and how to do an Eskimo roll. Fitting the spray deck firmly over the cockpit, Glen turned the kayak through a complete circle by rolling the kayak right over. One moment he was upside-down underwater and the next coming up for air on the other side.

"If you reckon you're going to capsize, pull this tab and it will release your spray deck. Then you won't be trapped inside the kayak."

Alex nodded casually.

Ten minutes later Glen was trying not to show his frustration, for Alex got every manoeuvre right first time. "Have you been in a kayak before?" he asked suspiciously.

"No," said Alex firmly. "Never in my life."

Glen felt a sapping of his own confidence. Was he going to be able to hold his own against Alex? Then he remembered that he was going to take him through the white water and felt better. Surely Alex wouldn't be able to deal with that? Glen had another satisfying mental picture of rescuing him, soaked and humiliated, after he'd capsized.

Glen gazed down the placid waters of the creek and was reminded yet again of how life had been with Dad before Kate and Alex had arrived. He'd tried so hard to get rid of them, but nothing he did seemed to have any effect.

Glen wanted a row, but to his irritation, Kate rode out all his verbal attacks, sometimes amused, sometimes sad, but always in control – just like Alex, who never challenged Glen and always remained seemingly calm and good-humoured no matter what happened.

Even his father had been getting on Glen's nerves lately, when he tried to be understanding. Glen found his comments deeply patronising and they only fuelled his anger.

"Look, Glen, I know it's difficult, but your mum, God bless her, died a long time ago. I've been really lonely." Dad sounded bluff and over-hearty, as if the pain of her death was something he'd never put behind him.

"You've got me," said Glen pugnaciously. "So how

come you've been so lonely?"

Glen had always been afraid that his father secretly blamed him for his mother's death. But in fact, Jon was unaware that Glen had never ceased to blame himself. Sometimes Glen dreamt she hadn't died, but was standing beckoning to him from the front doorstep of a house in a deep, dark, rustling forest. Although Glen had seen photographs of her, the figure of his mother in his dream always remained in shadow. As he got nearer to the front door, longing to feel her arms around him at last, she always vanished.

"Are you OK?" asked Alex, jerking Glen back to the present.

"Let's go." Glen pushed off his kayak from the bank and began paddling swiftly down the creek, leaving his pupil behind, heading fast for the river.

As Glen paddled his thoughts turned again to Kate. She had had what his father called a "messy" divorce from her first husband, and now Kate and Alex apparently never saw him. Why couldn't she have hung on to her husband? thought Glen impatiently. Why did she have to come and steal his father?

Glen slowed down as he came to the bend in the creek before it split into two channels, one of which would carry them on down to the main river that flowed through the forest. The trees – he shuddered as he imagined them hemming him in.

Glen remembered flying low over the dense mass of trees in the plane that had brought them to the small airstrip at Glengary and how he had shuddered at the sinister sight. He had also felt ashamed. This wasn't even the pine forest of his dreams – that dark, deathly place with its thick carpet of needles. The forest in this part of Canada also had some deciduous trees. There were also places where trees had been cut down in great swathes to make firebreaks. They gave a much more open feeling to this forest.

On the very first night in the lodge, Glen had had yet another disturbing dream. This time he was slowly walking up to the front door of the mysterious house in the forest where his mother lived.

In the dream, there was no sign of her, but the door was open and he ran through it – only to discover the house was completely empty. This emptiness seemed terrifying and made Glen feel hollow inside.

He had woken up sweating. In the light of day the dreams always seemed so stupid and babyish that he never dared confide them to anyone.

Glen turned his kayak so that he could see how Alex was getting on, and saw to his annoyance that he was only a few metres behind him, paddling smoothly, fully in control. Well, he'd soon change all that!

"Come on, Alex!" Glen shouted, as if Alex had been lagging behind rather than keeping pace with him. "You're getting the idea, but you shouldn't shove your paddle in so deep. You're slowing yourself down."

In fact Alex hadn't been doing anything of the kind and had been paddling along with a natural, easy rhythm, but Glen wasn't going to admit that.

"Sorry." Alex seemed to take his criticism to heart, checking his paddling, and Glen felt a sense of power. He'd got a reaction out of Alex at last. As they came to the fork in the creek, Glen began to paddle his way down the left-hand section into the river, aware of his growing desire to take risks.

Now was the time for the final reckoning, he

thought. He'd soon wipe that self-satisfied smirk off Alex's face.

"Hang on," said Alex.

"What's the matter?"

Alex came abreast of him and rafted up, bringing his kayak alongside and holding on to the side of Glen's. "I've been wondering – should we go through the white water? Didn't your dad say—"

"I told you, he was only being cautious. Don't you want to have some fun?"

"What about the falls?" asked Alex.

"They're miles further down. You scared, or something?" asked Glen belligerently.

"No." Alex seemed surprised. "Why should I be?"

"I mean, if you are, just say so." Glen was enjoying sounding superior.

"I'm not." Alex still sounded genuinely surprised. "I just don't want to deliberately disobey your dad."

"We can safely paddle through the rapids until we see the chains and the danger signs. We have to keep away from the chains. Do you understand?"

"Of course," replied Alex.

He really is scared, thought Glen hopefully, although

he knew in his heart that Alex was just talking good sense. But Glen didn't want to hear it. He wanted to humiliate Alex to such an extent that he would persuade his mother not to have anything more to do with the Barrons.

Extreme Danger

Friday, 12pm

"Come on." Glen was paddling towards the rapids. "Or are you chicken?" He didn't wait for a reply, but simply paddled on without looking back, although he was curious to know what Alex would do. Would he follow without further argument, or would he stay where he was? Glen longed to look over his shoulder, but didn't, knowing that would be a sign of weakness.

For a moment the enormity of what he was doing struck him, but Glen hurriedly pushed it into the background.

All at once the river broadened out and all Glen could see was spray. He gave an uneasy cheer and then gasped as Alex passed him, paddling rhythmically and looking not only able, but confident as well.

Soon they were both paddling in the shallow rapids, dodging the occasional rock, easily staying afloat.

"This is great!" shouted Alex, and Glen was amazed and annoyed that he was coping so well. And he even sounded happy! This was not what he'd planned at all.

The water was moving much faster now and in no time Alex was nearing the chain across the river. He turned his kayak all too expertly against the current and returned to Glen, but Glen ignored him, ducking under the chain and paddling his kayak swiftly past the warning notices. He felt a heady sensation of superiority. Alex would *have* to get riled now, and show him some of the real feelings that must lurk somewhere under that smooth, cheerful exterior.

"Are you crazy?" yelled Alex. "What did you do that for? Come back!"

"I just want to see what the deeper rapids are like," Glen shouted. "Want to come, or are you too scared?"

"Come back!" bellowed Alex. "Like now!"

But Glen was too preoccupied to reply. The current was tugging at his kayak and sweeping him ahead with alarming speed.

Alex pulled up the chain, ducked under and paddled fast towards Glen. But he couldn't close the distance between them.

Anxiously, Glen dug in his paddle to act as a brake so that he could slow up the kayak. "This is brilliant!" he yelled, determined not to show any fear, but in fact he was beginning to panic, aware that he was being swept round the bend of the river. Although he had turned the kayak, there seemed no way of slowing it down.

"Paddle harder!" shouted Alex from far behind him. "You'll be swept away!"

"I can't." Glen was finally scared. Suddenly his wind-up had gone wrong and now he was all too aware of the danger he was in. Why had he been so stupid?

"Paddle harder!" repeated Alex, getting closer to Glen now.

"I told you, I can't!"

They were both in the current now, and although Alex desperately tried to paddle against it, he soon realised he couldn't.

"You idiot!" Glen shouted. "Why did you come under the chain?"

"I was going to ask you the same thing!"

The current swept them on, both their kayaks spinning, and Glen realised if they paddled any harder they'd capsize. The falls, he thought with dread in his heart. They can't be far away!

"What do we do?" yelled Alex. For the first time he looked afraid, but Glen didn't feel the slightest sense of triumph, as by now he was terrified himself. Worse still, he knew he had already shown himself up to Alex. A dreadful humiliation filled him. What was he going to do now? He'd got them both into this mess, but how was he going to get them out of it?

As they were whirled around the bend in the river, Glen realised they were being pulled downstream at an even more furious rate, and the harder he tried to hold the kayak steady the more his kayak spun round.

What had he done? He'd never live this down. He'd deliberately disobeyed his father's instructions and put their lives at risk. What was the matter with him?

Glen glanced back at Alex who was shouting something he couldn't hear, his features twisted in terror. Suddenly he was no longer a blank page, no longer cool or laid-back. Glen had got what he wanted – but he didn't want it after all.

Trying desperately to keep his kayak steady, Glen could see that the river was narrowing into a gorge, the sheer sides lined with trees, like a deadly green army.

The darkness loomed above him, increasing Glen's fear as the current rushed him and Alex on, their kayaks spinning out of control, any attempt at steering with their paddles useless. By now the danger was very great, but Glen wasn't thinking about his own safety. All he could think of was Alex. Suppose he drowned? Glen could be up on a manslaughter charge – and deservedly so. Now all his anger, his desire to punish and humiliate, had vanished.

He thought all this in a split-second, but as the gorge gradually became narrower, Glen's attention was forced back to the struggle to keep his rocking kayak steady. The churning water surged forward faster and faster until a loud booming sound could be heard in the distance. The falls.

Glen felt sick with terror. There was nothing he could do, nothing at all; they were both going to die. He knew that they stood no chance of survival; they would either be dashed against the rocks or trapped under their overturned kayaks.

But, for a while, both Glen and Alex miraculously stayed upright. Glen's luck ran out first as his kayak hit a rock and overturned. He unclipped his spray deck and pressed his hands hard against the sides of the cockpit, hoping against hope that Alex was doing the same. Had he told him how to escape from his kayak if the fragile craft overturned? Glen couldn't remember. He couldn't remember *anything* he had told Alex.

Glen burst out of his kayak like a cork from a bottle and then felt himself truly in the grip of the current, hurtling along, driven bruisingly against the rocks, almost deafened by the booming of the falls. Desperately, he looked back, but couldn't see Alex anywhere. Then suddenly he was whirling past Alex, who'd also lost his kayak. Glen noticed there was a dark patch of blood on his forehead and felt a chill of horror. Was Alex already dead? But then he saw his arms flailing about as he attempted to swim and heard him shouting something, although the thundering of the falls was now so loud that there was no possible chance of hearing him.

As the current swept them on, Glen saw a cloud of spray and guessed they must be nearing the falls. Again, he glanced round, looking for Alex, and saw him hanging on to a rock, hugging the slippery surface as tightly as he could. Glen grabbed at another and also hung on to it, but he could feel the current tugging at him. Then his hands scrabbled at the rough surface and slipped away. He saw that Alex had let go too. They were both going to be swept over the falls, thought Glen. There could be no doubt about that now. But at least Alex had managed to unclip his spray deck and wasn't trapped under his kayak. He must have told him how to do it after all. But this was only a small comfort.

Moments later he saw an unbelievably frightening sight as the river just fell away. The panic hit Glen again and again. This was it – he'd never see Dad again. He'd never...

Still spinning, Glen was propelled over the falls and

suddenly his whole world narrowed down to a desperate attempt to survive. For a few moments Glen had the bizarre sensation of flying. But then he felt a sharp pain and he was in the thick of it, being swept over the rocks by the water, gasping and spitting it out, desperate not to drown.

Glen suddenly realised his life jacket and rucksack were helping to protect him as he continued to bounce off the rocks. Then he was toppled head-down and felt a dull thud as he seemed to rush into a spiralling tunnel of darkness.

Later, Glen found himself whirling along, not knowing where he was, the current pushing him on. The water was much deeper now and Glen was able to turn on his back and gaze up at the sunlight gleaming in a cloudless sky. He was amazed he had survived. Time seemed to be on hold. Glen realised he must have been unconscious and that he had no idea how long he had been in the water.

Birds flew across the face of the sun as the river broadened and gradually slowed, but Glen was now too exhausted to do anything but float. Amazingly, his rucksack was still strapped to his back.

Suddenly a feeling of elation swept him. Had he actually survived? Now the grip of the river was not so strong, maybe he could try to swim for the shore. Turning over on to his front, Glen began a limp crawl. But his elation was swept away abruptly as he remembered Alex. There was no sign of him.

And then he suddenly saw him standing on the bank, complete with rucksack, hands on knees, head down, clothes torn, blood dribbling down his face.

Panic-stricken, Glen forced himself to swim more strongly in spite of his bruised body. Would he be able to reach Alex? And if he did, would he be able to land?

Glen increased his speed and, to his surprise, soon reached the shore, hanging on to a tuft of grass, whispering Alex's name, knowing he didn't have the strength to drag himself up on to the bank. But the elation had returned because, in spite of everything, they were both alive.

For a long time Alex didn't seem to hear him calling and Glen, hanging on to the riverbank by his fingertips, began to shiver violently.

"Alex—"

Alex didn't look up.

"Help me!"

Still Alex stood on the bank as if turned to stone, hands on his knees, looking down.

"For God's sake, Alex!"

Finally he glanced in Glen's direction and looked away again.

"You've got to help me!"

Alex glanced at him again and then began to walk slowly over towards him.

"Hurry up!" Glen was shaking so much that his grip on the wiry grass was weakening.

Alex moved a little faster and looked down at Glen with anger and contempt. Reluctantly, he grabbed one of Glen's wrists, and with surprising strength pulled him on to the bank where he lay, gasping like a floundering fish.

Alex sank down to his knees beside him, watching Glen, rage flickering in his eyes. "You utter idiot," he said quietly. "You wanted to kill me."

This was a new side of Alex. Glen didn't know what to say. He couldn't reply.

"Didn't you?"

"I'm sorry."

"Is that all you can say?"

"I – I'm really sorry."

"You took this risk – this incredibly stupid risk – just to wind me up. Am I right? Or did you actually set out to kill me?"

Glen felt the full force of Alex's rage. "OK," he said, trying to take a grip on himself. "I took a risk and—"

"You're a complete fool. You're pathetic."

Glen knew he deserved Alex's contempt, but still felt a trace of his former elation. Didn't Alex realise how lucky they were – what a miracle their survival was? Despite what he, Glen, had done?

"You just wanted to show me up!" Alex was gazing down at him in astonishment and fury.

"Hang on," said Glen. "You agreed to come." Then a burst of honesty swept his truculence away. "You're right. I did want to wind you up."

"In the most dangerous way possible."

Glen nodded.

"You could have killed us both."

"I didn't think." Glen looked back at the river flowing past them, still at some speed. "Actually, I *did* think. I didn't want you around. Dad and I have been together a long time. I don't like strangers."

"Mum and I have been together for a long time too," said Alex bitterly. "My father walked out on us."

Glen paused, still gasping. He hadn't realised this. But why should he? Alex had never given away anything personal before. But then Glen had never considered him as a person – only as a threat. Tears filled Glen's eyes. As he tried to blink them away, he got as angry as Alex.

"My mother died. She died giving birth to me. You just try and imagine what that's like!" Glen's words were tumbling over each other, fighting to get out. He needed to confess after the enormity of what had happened, of what he'd done.

They were silent for a long while. Then Alex asked, "Did you *want* me to drown?"

"*No.*"

"Are you sure?"

Glen nodded. He suddenly realised that hating someone, like hating Kate and Alex, could also mean

they were important to him, important enough to hate.
"I'm sure. I told you – it was just meant to be a wind-up."
Glen paused. "I loathed you so much – you and your
mother. Didn't you feel it?"

"Mum told me to ignore all the hassle. She hoped
you'd come round if we didn't make a fuss. But you've
hurt her a lot."

"I didn't ask your mother to come. I didn't ask either
of you—" Again Glen felt suddenly close to hot and
angry tears.

"You didn't think that I felt the same way?" asked
Alex. "I can't stand you! I hate this situation!" Alex
glared at him ferociously and wiped at the blood that
was still oozing from the cut on his forehead.

Events had shaken Alex up and behind that shiny
protective surface Glen had at last seen the real person.

And the real Alex wasn't so very different from the
real Glen. They both had similar problems – a parent to
protect, a parent to mourn or miss. But now Glen had
finally realised that, it was too late. Although he didn't
need to hate him any more, Alex had said he couldn't
stand him.

They sat in silence on the bank.

"How far did we get carried down the river?" Alex asked eventually.

"I don't know."

"A few miles?"

"Quite a few miles."

"So we'd better start hiking."

"What about your head?" Glen struggled to his feet. "It's still bleeding a bit."

"I'm OK," said Alex impatiently.

He clearly wasn't. But Glen didn't think he could argue with him.

"How long will it take us to get back?" Alex went on. "Let's have a look at the map."

Glen dragged out the map of the National Park, but it was impossible to find out where they had landed. The map wasn't small scale, and even if it had been they still couldn't be sure how far down the river they'd been swept. Dad hadn't bargained on them accidentally shooting the falls, thought Glen miserably. They were in big trouble. He wondered what Dad would say – if they even managed to survive. He winced as he imagined his father's angry disappointment in him.

Suddenly Alex gave a cry of triumph. "Hang about!"

He was looking down at his wrist. "This beats the adverts."

"What does?" asked Glen.

"My shockproof watch. It's still going."

"More than mine is," said Glen regretfully, gazing down at his own. The glass was smashed and it was obviously ruined.

"What's more," said Alex, "I can use my watch as a compass. It's one thirty and we've been heading north-east. We want to get back south. Look – there's the salmon spawning channel on the map. We can work our way back to the cabin from there all right. Those falls we fell down – they're marked on here too. I think they're about halfway back home."

Glen looked at the map and for once forgot to try to be superior. "Well done," he said warmly. "So we just follow the hands of the watch—"

"And when they're at twenty to two..." Alex's voice petered out. "Wait a minute. I'm not sure I remember how to do this."

Glen was under such stress that he immediately lost his temper. "*Why* don't you know?"

"Why didn't you know how close we were to the

falls?" Alex replied sarcastically. "OK, I forgot – you wanted to wind me up."

There was a long, hostile silence.

"We have to be really careful," Glen said eventually, swaying slightly, feeling incredibly weak, his body bruised. Cuts he hadn't realised he'd got were hurting badly all of a sudden. "You've – we've got to remember this is bear country. We've got to get back somehow. And quickly."

Alex stared at him. "Did your dad suspect you were going to defy him and go out on the white water?"

"You know he didn't."

"So he's not going to organise a search party."

"Not yet. Not till this evening, I suppose."

"And even when he does, he won't have a clue where to start looking."

Glen didn't reply, gazing out at the dense forest that swept down to the river. How were they going to get back? He shuddered. Which was worse? The river or the forest? The forest won, hands down. But were they going to get back at all?

Lost

"I'll get you back to the lodge,"

said Glen. "I'll get you back somehow." But he didn't feel very confident as he looked around them. There was nothing to tell him which way they should go. He also felt numb, still unable to believe his own crass stupidity. What would Dad say? What would Kate say? But he knew. Alex had already said it all.

"You're the last person I'm going to rely on."

"OK," said Glen woodenly, unable to get a grip on the situation. He looked at the dense trees and thought for the first time of bears. How big a problem were they going to be? But Glen still knew his biggest problem would be finding the way back. Even then he would have to face his father.

"Wait a minute," said Alex. "I'm beginning to remember."

"What?"

"How to use my watch as a compass."

"So how do you use it?" Glen hated sounding so dependent.

"I was wrong the first time."

This was the first time Alex had had to admit he was wrong and Glen noticed that he didn't find it particularly hard – not nearly as hard as Glen himself would have.

"OK." Alex was very calm. "Point the hour hand at the sun. Then divide the angle between the hour hand and the twelve to find south. We need to keep south to get back. And look at the map again. Doesn't it show the Six Sisters – six rocky islands in a row? I think we passed them."

"I don't remember."

"I do." Alex got out the map again. "See where they

are? That must mean we've travelled at least thirty miles downriver."

"As much as that?"

"Maybe even a little more," said Alex.

"I reckon the best thing to do is to follow the river upstream," suggested Glen, needing to take the initiative. "Even with your watch it would be stupid to try and take any short cuts."

"I think you're right." Alex seemed generous and suddenly Glen wanted to repay his generosity.

"But how easily *can* we follow the river back?"

"We may need to go into the forest a bit. But then we can use my watch to make sure we're still heading in the right direction."

Glen shuddered. Going into the forest a bit was still his idea of hell.

Along the riverbank the going was difficult. Several times, their path blocked by dense undergrowth, Glen and Alex were forced to make detours into the darkness of the closely packed trees.

Glen was worried that if they went too deep into the forest, even with Alex's watch as their compass, they could easily get lost. They were also stiff and sore after their ordeal, bruised and cut by the rocks.

"This could take weeks," grumbled Alex. "And we haven't got any food or water."

"Yes we have! We've still got the picnic in the rucksacks. It should be OK." Glen dragged off his rucksack and looked at his share of the picnic doubtfully. It had seemed far too much when Kate had given it to him; now it seemed too little. "We'll have a quick snack," he said. "It'll give us more energy."

There was a long silence as they started to weave in and out of the trees again, making very little progress, but Glen was so numb, so shocked at what he had done, that he felt a sense of unreality about their plight.

Alex, however, was unable to stop his anger. "There's no trail. Nothing!"

"What did you expect? Signposts? A bus service? A taxi rank?"

"What I'm trying to tell you," snarled Alex, "is this. It's not only really difficult to keep the river in sight while we're weaving in and out of the trees, but at this rate we're never going to get back! Where are we, anyway?"

Not answering Alex – what was there to say? – Glen pressed forward amongst the dark trees, a strong feeling of claustrophobia spreading over him. His sense of unreality was beginning to be replaced by one of fear.

Glen tried to calm himself by noting that he could still just see the river, glinting through the trees, but soon he became convinced that in the silence of the forest he could now hear snapping twigs behind him. At first he told himself firmly that it must be Alex. But when Glen allowed himself to stop and turn round he realised, to his horror that, although Alex *was* immediately behind him, he was standing stock-still. The ominous sounds had to be coming from somewhere behind them both.

"What's that?" Glen hissed.

"I don't know."

The snapping sound continued and then stopped, making the ensuing silence even more uncomfortable.

"What's going on?" whispered Alex. "What are we stopping for?"

"Shut up!" said Glen in a fierce whisper.

The elk stole into the small glade, listening intently.

The creature was exquisitely beautiful, with a long, lean body that had grey markings. It looked a bit like a reindeer but bigger. Was it their presence the elk could sense? Or was there something else? The snapping sound came again – and there was rustling in the undergrowth.

Normally a shy creature like this would have noticed them and run away, thought Glen. So why was the elk hanging around? He had the unsettling feeling that they were all under some kind of enchantment, that time had been suspended. Yet the tension was rising as if he was pulling an elastic band as hard as he could, knowing it was going to break, but not knowing when.

Glen could hear himself breathing, could feel his heart racing, thumping hard and painfully. Then he heard yet another sound and froze. Danger was near. They should move. But Glen couldn't. He had a strange feeling that if they all stood very still and didn't say the word "bear", it wouldn't actually appear.

Glen glanced at Alex to see that he *was* rigidly still, only a little pulse in his temple giving away how terrified he was.

If we don't move, thought Glen, nothing can

happen. The world can stay on hold.

Suddenly, without the slightest warning, a larger elk, complete with huge antlers – a male – detached itself from the shadows, trotting across the glade and snuffling at what Glen thought must be the female.

Again Glen glanced at Alex who was gazing transfixed at the two shy creatures. They made a particularly beautiful sight.

The boys continued to stand absolutely still, trying not to move or draw attention to themselves. But Glen's mouth was painfully dry and the crazy temptation to clear his throat was overwhelming. All he wanted to do in the world was to cough. He just about managed to control himself, concentrating on the elks which had suddenly frozen, listening intently to something neither of the boys could hear.

The silence seemed to deepen and Glen was intensely aware that they were out of their element, in an alien wilderness, a place where they were unwelcome. Although they had survived the falls, he felt that the forest was going to make every attempt to see they didn't survive much longer.

In the continued unsettling silence, Glen began to

feel as if he was being watched...by a bear. He remembered how Dad had told him the bears were timid and were unlikely to attack. But surely that was only true of bears in civilisation? The forest wasn't civilisation. It was bear country.

We shouldn't be here, thought Glen as the dread feeling of being watched intensified.

The elks remained still, sniffing the air curiously. What was happening, wondered Glen. *Could* they smell bear?

The waiting was terrible. Glen was still rigid, hardly daring to breathe, and he was sure that Alex was feeling the same. At any moment the bear might charge out of the undergrowth and rip out their throats with his enormous teeth. Maybe they only had moments to live. Again Glen remembered his father's words. "The grizzlies are scared of human beings. They wouldn't attack unless they were starving – or their cubs were threatened." But could he and Alex be threatening their cubs by their very presence in the forest?

Then the two elks seemed to emerge from their trance, and with a light brushing sound ran off and were swallowed up by the dark trees.

But Glen and Alex were still too afraid to move. They remained on the edge of the glade, staring fearfully into the shadows.

We could be here all night, thought Glen. Determined to make a decision he began to back away, bumping into a tree, cursing, and falling to the ground. But at least no bear had appeared and turned his fears into reality.

"You idiot!" hissed Alex, striding after Glen and looking at him in fury.

Glen scrambled to his feet, but Alex was already heading back in the direction of the river.

After what seemed a very long and tense walk through the trees they arrived back at the river bank. To Glen's dismay he saw that they couldn't simply follow the river because the path ahead of them disappeared into dense rocky undergrowth.

"We'll have to push our way through that lot," said Glen, trying to be positive. "If we tough it out, we won't have to go back into the forest."

He plunged into the undergrowth and tried to make progress. But he made none. It was as if the forest had suddenly come alive, as if it had a central brain and thousands of different limbs, like vines and creepers, thorns and tangles, all of which were wrapping round him at once. Losing his temper, Glen began to struggle, kicking and tearing at the undergrowth and rocky boulders, but they refused to give way.

Alex, who had been tactfully silent at first, began to snort with laughter, and then to emit peal after peal.

Glen turned on him with bunched fists. "Why don't you shut up?" he yelled, but Alex laughed all the harder.

"How on earth can we get through that lot?" Alex asked eventually. His mood had changed. The hysteria was over.

"We can't," said Glen, suddenly needing to be truthful, to stop fooling himself as well as Alex. If they were going to survive they had to be completely realistic, however painful that was. "But we've got to take some decisions, like when we're going to eat next – and whether we're going to try and get back home before dark – or make camp."

"If you hadn't been so stupid, we wouldn't have to

make these decisions!" Alex was suddenly furious with him again.

"There's no point in going over that now." Glen was gaining a little more confidence. "We need to think what we're going to do next."

"Don't you preach at me!" Alex shouted and punched Glen hard in the chest.

Instinctively, Glen hit him back, and despite his size he put so much power into the punch that he knocked Alex to the ground.

Alex got up and threw himself on Glen and they both crashed into the undergrowth, nearly rolling into the river, then springing apart.

"You stupid fool," said Glen.

They both listened to the small scurrying sounds of the forest and Glen felt an increasing certainty that they were still being watched. There was a long silence as he felt the claustrophobia of the forest begin to smother him. The trees seemed to be coming nearer, stalking him like bears, rustling their leaves and branches. Perhaps he was still in shock. He had to get a grip on himself.

To his surprise, Alex then said, "I'm sorry. I lost control."

"You always lose control if you hate someone enough. Look what I did on the river." Glen was amazed that he was able to speak so frankly. A few hours ago he would never have been capable of such honesty. He felt a little better, a little less hemmed in.

"Yes. I can see that."

"We've still got to take decisions, like whether we're going to camp or not. I'm hungry and thirsty. How about you?"

"Of course I am," snapped Alex. "I don't think we should try to make camp. We can walk all night if necessary. How long do you think the journey will take?"

"How do I know?" Glen paused. "I don't think we've made much progress. But it's hard to tell. Probably the best thing to do *is* to keep moving. I reckon we'll make the lodge by tonight." He tried to sound positive, but was sure he only sounded childishly hopeful.

"Our folks are going to be out of their minds with worry." Alex's voice wobbled.

"I know."

"And then there's the bears—"

"Sure."

"If we meet one, we're completely defenceless."

Glen suddenly realised that he would have to help to rally Alex if they were going to survive. "I'm really sorry about what I did. I had no right to get you into this mess and it's all my fault, OK? We probably won't meet any bears – their territories are so large. But we've got to get back – and the quicker we make a proper start the better."

Alex nodded, and without any more discussion the boys began to trudge back into the forest, trying to get round the rocky undergrowth by the side of the river. As they struggled on, Glen in the lead, Alex gloomily plodding along behind him, he felt increasingly conscious of the small scurryings around them, and was sure Alex felt the same. Was the bear waiting for them? Watching? Hiding? Ready to pounce? Once again, Glen told himself that bears rarely attacked humans. Unless they were hungry. Or afraid.

"We've *got* to sit down and eat," said Alex suddenly. Glen was glad he hadn't been the first to say that. He simulated reluctance and then began to open his rucksack. "We'll just have a snack," said Alex. "We need to conserve the food. We have to think of the worst case scenario. We could be out here for days."

They sat down and opened the containers. There was ham and cheese and lots of bread and fruit. Glen felt grateful towards Kate for the first time ever.

They both began to tear at the food, forgetting the word "snack", until Alex said, "We'd better slow down. And we'll have to ration the water. We can't drink the river water. It'll be full of bacteria and that would be the end of any survival plans we've got."

Reluctantly, Glen stopped eating and with considerable regret put Kate's picnic back in his rucksack.

They plodded along without exchanging a word for over an hour. Gradually, Glen's hopes of getting back to the lodge that evening began to decrease, but surprisingly, the silence between himself and Alex had become more comfortable. Was it a kind of truce? Or just mutual exhaustion? Probably, the trouble would begin when they started talking again.

Slowly, Glen and Alex found a way back to the river again, and discovered the undergrowth was no longer completely barring they way. The current was slow so they knew they must still be some considerable distance from the falls. Glen also knew that when they eventually reached the falls they would somehow have to climb around them, and conditions would get even more difficult. But despite all this, Glen still longed to see the falls. The way back seemed interminable. They must have been swept downriver much further than he had imagined.

Slowly, the sun set and the moon rose, giving the river an eerie glow, milky and insubstantial. But soon the bank began to widen and the trees seemed less threatening, less dense. At last they were able to walk side by side, shivering a little in the chill night air.

"I don't like this," blurted out Glen. Then he swore at himself inwardly for being stupid enough to give Alex another chance to put him down.

"I wouldn't say I was having a ball," replied Alex. "I feel as if someone has picked me up and thrown me at a brick wall. I've never felt so sore."

"I don't mean that." Glen was impatient. "It's the forest. It feels like a living thing – a living organism…" He let his words die away, all too certain he was making a fool of himself.

There was a silence as they tramped on, so long that Alex tried to come to the rescue.

"You don't need to worry about a bunch of stupid trees," he said clumsily. "It's the bears we need to look out for. They're probably watching us now."

"It's like the trees are moving in." Glen shivered. "We're not wanted out here." Then he came to a stumbling halt.

"Are you going off your head?" Alex sounded more concerned than angry.

"No," said Glen as firmly as he could. If Alex thought he'd begun to crack up then he wasn't surprised. "I just think there are certain places you shouldn't disturb."

"I know what you mean," said Alex, and Glen turned to stare at him in amazement. Surely Alex couldn't actually be agreeing with him, or understand a fear that must seem so alien. "We're out of our element. Humans are really puny when they're out in the wild."

"Don't you mean *I'm* really puny?" Glen was immediately on the defensive again. Then he wondered why he had to try and prove himself all the time. It was such hard work.

"I didn't say that. What are you on about?" Alex looked at him anxiously and for the first time Glen felt a spark of warmth between them. Alex seemed determined to placate him, to prevent another quarrel.

"I don't know. It's just my size I suppose. I've always been small for my age."

"You shouldn't let—" Alex broke off as he gazed ahead. "Just look at that."

"What's the matter?" Glen felt irritated again. "You make everything sound like an emergency."

"There *is* an emergency," said Alex, his voice harsh with fear. "Can't you see the smoke?"

No Smoke Without Fire

Friday, just before 12am

"Smoke? What smoke?"

But now Glen could see the distant dark cloud billowing up into the sky. He wondered why he was trying to deny its existence. Was it because he couldn't take any more? Couldn't he cope with the fact that his stupidity had landed them in a situation where absolutely everything was loaded against them? The new understanding he had with Alex seemed blown away. Hardly surprising, when it was so fragile.

"The forest's on fire!" gasped Alex.

"That's all we need," muttered Glen.

But the fire seemed quite a long way off. Glen and Alex watched in silence, trying to assess what a long way off really was.

"Do you think the fire's coming our way?" asked Glen.

"How would I know?" Alex sounded deeply depressed – and very afraid.

Glen tried to defuse the situation. "Well, I suppose the smoke must be quite far away. We haven't reached the falls yet, and it looks even further off than that. It's only a smudge in the sky," he continued, realising that what he'd said to comfort Alex was probably true. But he also remembered Dad telling him that the forest was very dry and this was the start of the high-risk season for fires. "What can be done?" Glen had asked, and his father's familiar voice came painfully into his mind. *"They've tried everything. Widening the firebreaks, warning the public, making more reservoirs. But nothing stops the fires breaking out and the animals are seriously at risk. They head for the river. It's their only escape route."*

"Say something helpful," snapped Alex, sounding

childishly demanding, breaking into Glen's anxious thoughts.

"Dad told me there's a high fire risk in the summer and there's not a lot that can be done." Glen paused uneasily and then added, "He says the animals head for the river."

"Bears, for instance?" Alex sounded hopeless, as if this new setback was too much for him. "I don't call that information very helpful."

"I'm sure the fire is still a long way in front of us," repeated Glen with a confidence he didn't feel.

"So we're walking straight into it," said Alex flatly, clearly not finding Glen very comforting.

"We could be back at the lodge before the fire reaches anywhere near us, but if not – we'll have to get round it somehow," replied Glen. He felt contempt for his lack of clarity, for his inability to lead. He had plunged them both into a wilderness that might be near civilisation, but not near enough if such crass risks were taken.

"How?" asked Alex.

Glen had no answer and they trudged on again in silence. They seemed worlds apart now, almost as if they were each inhabiting a different world.

Then Alex blurted out fearfully, "The bears will be pushed in our direction, won't they? They'll be fleeing the fire – and finding us. Those bears could be starving, hungry enough to eat human flesh."

"I still think they'll be too afraid to attack us, and staying by the river is definitely the best way to find our way back." Glen tried to sound authoritative.

"Still, you couldn't have bogged things up at a worse time, could you?" said Alex drily, needing to attack, not attempting to reach Glen any more, as if he had run out of that kind of energy.

Glen could only agree. Then he tried again. "Look – Dad told me forest fires don't travel more than half-a-mile to a mile in an hour. The smoke doesn't look as if it's that close – it could be as much as thirty miles away. The fire could even burn out before it reaches us."

"Let's hope your dad's right," snapped Alex.

Again Glen felt an optimistic fool, as if he was playing a game. This is for real, he told himself. The bears might be a danger, but so was starvation. So was getting burnt to death.

*

They trekked on, the river at last flowing faster as they slowly and painfully trudged up the never-ending climb to the falls. But Glen couldn't see them or hear that great thundering of the mass of water yet. Once again he realised how far the current had propelled them downriver. He must have been unconscious for a long time. Too long to be able to assess the distance between where they were now, and where the "accident" had happened.

Soon the undergrowth became dense again. Now Glen and Alex had enormous difficulty in making progress, having to edge back into the dark shadows under the trees.

Glen immediately became intensely conscious of the sounds of the forest and was soon finding difficulty in trying to control his imagination. There were small scurrying sounds, an occasional high-pitched chattering, and, most ominous of all, much heavier sounds, as if they were being slowly but relentlessly pursued by unseen pounding grizzlies.

Glen gazed into the forest. Suddenly he thought he could hear the thundering of the falls, sounding like the roaring of some enormous primeval animal lost amongst the trees.

"What's that?" rasped Alex suddenly.

"What's what?"

"I thought I heard something. Didn't you hear anything?"

"No." Glen was defiant. He didn't want to agree and then be found to be wrong. The shadows moved, taking on shifting forms, shapes that were made worse and more threatening by his over-sensitive imagination.

"You deaf or something?" Alex sounded belligerent, as if he expected, or even wanted, an argument.

"Could be." Glen's voice was dull and bleak.

They listened again, and then Alex said, "For God's sake, Glen, listen! That's the roaring of water. That's the roaring of the falls! Or have I got confused? Do you think we're hearing the roaring of bears?"

Glen listened and with a sudden lightening of his heart realised that Alex was right. They were listening to the falls. He let out a great whoop of joy – and then stopped, wondering why he'd been such a fool to make so much noise.

"Am I right?" asked Alex. "Or am I right!"

Glen gave him a mock punch on the arm. "You're right," he said. "You're absolutely right!"

"Come on," said Glen. "We've got to keep going. But let's have a quick drink first." Now he was thirsty. Really thirsty.

"I don't think we should." Glen thought that Alex sounded smug.

"Why not?" Glen's mouth was so dry he could hardly speak. "We've got a couple of bottles hardly touched."

"We've got one bottle – one litre bottle – each. Not quite a full litre. That's not much. We need to conserve supplies."

"So when do you think we should have a drink?"

"Not yet," said Alex with irritating pedantry.

"When?" croaked Glen.

"Maybe in an hour or so."

"OK."

Glen strode on with a mental image of Alex being eaten with relish by the largest grizzly bear possible. Maybe grizzlies *did* get stroppy, he thought. Right now he'd just love Alex to meet a stroppy bear!

*

They were both having trouble walking, but neither wanted to admit that to the other. Glen felt so sore and battered and bruised that every step was painful, especially as he'd cut his legs badly and the rough material of his Chinos was rubbing against the abrasions.

Then Alex seemed to relent. "You OK?"

"Kind of."

"What does that mean?"

"I'm badly cut about." Glen's voice shook and he suddenly realised he was within an ace of breaking down. It wasn't just the cuts. The prospect of the bears being driven towards them by the fire was more frightening than the fire itself. Suddenly Glen wanted to curl up in some dark place and hide until he was rescued. Even hiding in the depths of the forest seemed less threatening than carrying on walking in such exhaustion and pain.

He glanced at Alex, wondering how much he had given away, and was surprised to see he looked sympathetic.

"I know," said Alex. "It *is* painful to walk. I hurt all

over, and the cut on my head still aches. But we're lucky to be alive, to have survived that kind of...accident. If we can keep the river in sight, then we should get back in one piece. We can do it. Besides, we can hear the falls – and I think that roaring's coming nearer." Glen felt almost friendly towards Alex as he spoke. For once, he didn't feel patronised.

Glen decided to count his steps. He had reached five hundred when something made him turn. They were still climbing, albeit gently, towards the steep incline that led to the falls. But Glen knew there was a long way to go yet.

Alex had stopped too, and was looking around nervously. "Come on," gasped Glen. "We'll never make the lodge by morning at this rate."

"Listen." Alex sounded wary.

"What's the matter?"

"Ssh! I said – listen!"

Then Glen saw that a single shadow had detached itself from the darkness. What was it? The shadow was definitely a crouching shape and Glen heard a small whimpering sound. He began to sweat. Then the whimpering turned into a whine.

Again, time seemed to be on hold. Below them they could just make out the river through the trees as a strip of silver, the sky and the moon like a painted ceiling.

"It's a bear cub," whispered Alex.

Glen saw it now, about six metres away from them. The little bear seemed frozen in its tracks, like a badger cub Glen had once seen by the road in England, dazed by the headlights.

"It's only a cub," hissed Glen.

But Alex didn't reply. Deep down, Glen knew what they were both thinking: where there's a cub, there's bound to be a mother.

Moments later a larger and much bulkier shadow detached itself from the shelter of the trees and undergrowth. There was also a dense, rank smell so pungent that Glen almost gagged.

"Don't move, Alex," hissed Glen. "For God's sake, don't move." But he wasn't sure if Alex had heard him.

Then Alex froze, just as Glen had.

"Play dead," whispered Glen, throwing himself to the ground. But Glen looked up again suddenly as he heard the sound of running footsteps. To his horror, Alex had panicked and was running, sometimes stumbling, weaving his way in and out of the dark trees.

Now he was veering wildly to the right, *towards* the bear cub. He must be too scared to know what the hell he's doing, thought Glen, for he'd put himself between the mother bear and the cub!

The mother hesitated and then took off, pursuing her cub – and Alex. Her massive frame pounded after him, the ridge of fur over her shoulders rising, paws thumping the ground and making a low growling sound that was horribly aggressive.

"Stop running, Alex!" Glen shouted. "Drop down! I told you, play dead!"

To his intense relief, Alex changed direction. Using some last-minute instinct he ran under a group of densely packed trees and threw himself to the ground.

The bear hesitated and then ran past him, catching up with her cub, and in just a few seconds they were both lost in the darkness.

Only the rank smell remained.

Glen jumped up and stood stock-still, listening to the deep silence around him. Then the small scurrying sounds began again, as if every small creature had been just as frightened as they were. Glen found the sounds that had originally terrified him were now oddly comforting.

Glen walked slowly over to Alex.

He was lying in a foetal position at the base of a tree.

Glen knelt down beside him and gently took his arm.

"Are you all right?" he asked.

Alex didn't reply and Glen grabbed his shoulders and shook him. There was still no reaction.

"Alex – what's the matter? You've got to get up now. You're not hurt, are you?"

Panic began to fill Glen. Maybe Alex was dead. Maybe he'd died of fright – and then Glen would be alone amongst the deeply packed trees which to him seemed as threatening as the mother bear.

Suddenly Alex moved and sat up, shaking all over.

"I thought she was going to kill me," he croaked.

Glen felt a surge of relief. "She was only interested in protecting her cub," he whispered. "The trouble is, you were in the way."

"You know what? We can't cope out here!"

"We've got to."

"But we can't, and we won't." There was an edge of hysteria in Alex's voice that reminded Glen of his hysterical laughter earlier. The sound made Glen very afraid. Suppose Alex cracked up? Suppose he had to make a bivouac for Alex and leave him behind, stealing through the densely packed trees on his own? He'd never find the way. At least Alex had his watch that could double up as a compass – but then only he knew how to use the thing.

Then Glen tried to pull himself together. The noise of the falls was louder, surely much louder. Alex wasn't going to crack up. Glen wouldn't let him. They *had* to stay together. That was the only way they could survive.

"We'll be OK. If we keep moving," said Glen as reassuringly as he could.

But Alex was past reassurance, past words that meant nothing. "We don't have a—" he began despondently.

Glen lost all control and slapped Alex round the face

as hard as he could. He had to get Alex to snap out of this!

Alex got to his feet and Glen wondered if he was going to try and fight him again. He hoped he wasn't. They could destroy each other out here.

But Alex didn't seem to be responding aggressively. He simply looked humiliated. Wasn't this what he had originally wanted? thought Glen. Hadn't he hoped to shock and humble him? Now he was achieving that, but in some nightmarish way.

"I'm sorry," said Glen.

"What for?"

"Slapping you."

"It's OK." Alex suddenly grinned at him, and to his relief Glen saw that he seemed to have got his grip back. "I needed a bit of a slap."

"You got it!"

"I completely lost my cool." Alex seemed embarrassed.

Glen laughed. "That's an understatement," he said. Then he added hurriedly, "Don't worry. You're not the only one! We're both scared out of our minds."

Alex began to tremble. Then he pulled himself

together with an effort. "Let's move on," he said.

"Are you sure?"

"What else can we do?"

"Have a drink," said Glen.

Alex looked as if he was going to refuse. Then he shrugged the rucksack off his shoulders and Glen did the same.

They got out the bottles and took a couple of swigs. The water was incredibly refreshing even though it was warm. Shakily, Glen grinned at Alex.

"What's so funny?" asked Alex.

"I was thinking how terrible it would have been if you'd died."

"So that's a bit of a joke, is it?"

"Don't be daft. I couldn't carry on alone. Besides, I–I'm glad you're OK. Really."

Alex shrugged. "You could carry on alone," he said grimly. "And you would. You'd get the instinct of survival."

"I think we've both got that already," said Glen.

Alex nodded. "If we work together we'll make it."

"I'm really sorry about the kayaking, about—" began Glen.

"Shut up!" said Alex. "If I hear you go on about that again, I'll kill you. And that'll mean more rations for me. So watch it!"

The Trees are Closing In

Glen trod cautiously into the pitch darkness of the trees. Unable to see where he was going, he kept bumping into trunks and branches which rustled against his face, sharp and brittle, as if they were already beginning to claw him. He smelt pine resin and felt the carpet of needles under his feet, soft and deep, dragging him down.

Glen's real and imagined fears began to merge. Dream and reality were almost one.

He felt like he did in his dreams. His mother had

vanished. He was getting lost. He'd never find his way back to safety again.

A night breeze filtered through the forest and the rustling intensified. Glen was shivering violently and trying to move as silently as possible. Suddenly he realised that was just what he shouldn't be doing. Dad had said creeping along was dangerous and threatening to the bears. If they knew where you were they would avoid you – and be less worried than if they were picking up a human scent that was silently coming closer and becoming a threat. Had the grizzly made off with her cub, or was she close by, waiting to pounce on him?

"What's the matter?" asked Alex.

Glen was startled. He'd felt so alone, he'd almost forgotten Alex was there with him. All their talk of working together had vanished from his head directly they got on the move again.

"I just don't like the forest."

"Because of the bears?"

"Not just because of the bears."

"What else then?" Alex's voice was much more gentle and sympathetic now.

"It's nothing."

"Tell me."

For some reason, maybe because he was exhausted, maybe because he'd thought for a moment that the bear had killed Alex and left him to wander on his own, Glen was desperate to confide in someone.

"Since my mother died when I was little – I've always had this weird idea she was lost in a forest."

"She didn't die in a forest, though, did she?"

Glen groaned. "No. I told you. She died giving birth to me. I just dream that she's got lost in a forest. That's all." Glen could almost hear Alex trying to understand – and failing. "It doesn't matter," he snapped. "Let's not talk about it."

"I'd like to understand." Alex sounded as if he really would, but Glen was no longer in the mood and he quickened his stride.

The smoke on the moonlit skyline had become wispy and faint and Glen began to feel a little more optimistic as they trudged upwards. But their slowly rising ascent, continuously broken by enforced detours, was frustratingly slow.

"We should make camp," said Alex suddenly, as they reached the thinning trees, closer to the river again. "It's far too dangerous to be wandering about like this at night." He sounded peevish and had come to a halt by an oak tree.

Now there were fewer pines around him, Glen felt less claustrophobic. But as he looked closely at the oak, he saw something strange. There was a series of marks on the bark, which were crossed by others in which black hairs and fur were embedded. There was something menacing about the marks, almost as if they were in some sort of code. Glen could see Alex gazing at them in dismay. Guessing what he was thinking, Glen tried to reassure him.

"They're claw marks," said Glen. "That's all they are."

"The bears know." Alex was beside himself with anxiety.

"Know what?"

"Where we are. They're telling each other. They're closing in on us!"

"Don't be ridiculous." But Glen was worried. Alex suddenly seemed to be losing his grip again.

"You'll see!" Alex gazed around, his eyes wild, and Glen had the terrible thought that he'd gone mad. "The fire's getting worse," he was saying, but he wasn't even looking in its direction.

"I don't think so." Glen tried to be reassuring, but only succeeded in sounding empty.

"In our state – without sleep – we could blunder into anything. Everyone knows that."

"You're just being negative," Glen snapped. "We can't just be negative – we can't afford to be, or we'll never get out of here!"

"What gives you the right to tell me what to do?"

"Have it your own way. I couldn't care less about what happens to you," hissed Glen.

There was a tense silence.

After a long time, Alex suddenly spoke. "Wait a minute – isn't this a clearing? Hasn't some logging been done here?"

Glen gazed around him in the darkness. "There's a stack of wood over there." Suddenly he felt more hopeful. Yet again. Glen was getting worried about his mood swings. They seemed so wild, so unpredictable, almost as if he had become a forest animal himself.

Alex was looking up. "The fire *is* getting nearer," he said.

Glen looked into the trees and realised he was right. The fire *was* slowly getting nearer. But it was still a long way ahead, just a grey smoke cloud on the horizon. Maybe the fire will burn itself out, thought Glen – although he couldn't think of a single reason why it should.

"I'm not actually sure we'll be able to get through that fire. So we'll have to try – have to come up with something." Glen hoped he sounded dynamic and resourceful, but he had a feeling he sounded like a wimp. "At some point our only alternative might be to get up the falls themselves, climbing up the rocks at the side where the water's shallower." Glen glanced at Alex, wondering if he was seeing the idea as a possibility.

"Are you mad?" said Alex. "We'd fall into the river and either drown or break our necks. And even if we didn't, we'd just get swept back and have to start all over again! What was that story? When some bloke had to push a boulder up a hill, but he never reached the top because the boulder kept rolling down again and he had to go on and on doing it for all eternity!" Alex's voice shook and Glen looked away.

As they pushed on in silence, Glen wondered if Alex was going to say they should stop and sleep. He wished he would. It had to be something like three in the morning and there could be no light of dawn for hours yet. Glen was so desperately tired that his rucksack was more of a dead weight than ever and his eyes kept closing. Several times he stumbled and almost fell, but Alex only plodded on, slowly, relentlessly, sometimes stumbling himself.

Resentfully, Glen followed, again acutely conscious of the noise of movement in the forest. Small scurryings had become a rush of paws. The sound of twigs cracking was far more frequent, almost like machine–gun fire, as if an army of animals was pushing its way through the trees. Glen began to wonder what had happened to the mother grizzly and her cub. Had they been trapped by the smoke and flames? Or were more of them heading their way, the females with frightened cubs that must be protected? And what about male grizzlies? They would be even more powerful, even more ferocious, and, because of the fire, even more unpredictable.

Absorbed in his thoughts, Glen tripped and almost fell again, just saving himself in time.

"I'm exhausted," he blurted out. "Maybe we should make a bivouac and get some sleep." But as he spoke, Glen imagined the frantic face of his beloved father, no doubt wondering if they had both drowned. The kayaks would have drifted way downstream by now and would give no clue to their whereabouts, or had probably been broken up by the falls. Would his dad even search the white water at all? Would he think for one minute that Glen could be so criminally stupid?

"I think we should keep walking." To Glen, Alex sounded censorious.

"I'm knackered."

"We can't lie down and sleep with that fire sweeping towards us – however far away it is."

Glen thought he detected a note of hesitancy in Alex's voice, though, and when he stole a glance at him he could see his face was haggard and drawn.

"We need sleep," said Glen decisively. "We can't go

on without rest. Just for a little while. We won't sleep for long."

They sat down and dragged out the tubs of food and bottles of water, rationing them carefully.

"I'll keep watch first," said Alex.

Glen nodded.

"I'll wake you up in an hour's time."

Packing away the tubs and making sure the rucksacks were secure, Glen lay down on the ground. Alex sat against the trunk of a tree.

"Night," said Alex to Glen, but he only received a snore in reply.

Glen dreamt of searching for his mother amongst the trees that grew so closely together that he was in total darkness. Then a moonbeam suddenly lit a small clearing. He ran into the glade hopefully, but was soon knee-deep in leaf mulch. As usual, there was no sign of her. Then a cloud passed over the moon and he was back in the suffocating darkness yet again.

Glen woke with a gasp.

"What the hell's the matter?"

"I was dreaming," Glen muttered. He gazed around him. A pale dawn was creeping across the sky and he wondered how long he'd slept. "Why didn't you wake me? You were meant to wake me!" Glen sounded childishly querrulous.

"I fell asleep too."

Glen felt relieved that he had not been the only one to crash out with exhaustion.

"I'm so hungry. What time do you reckon we'll make it back?" asked Alex.

"I don't know," replied Glen miserably.

"Surely you've got some idea?"

"Why should I? Have you?"

"You're useless," said Alex contemptuously, seeming to dismiss Glen completely.

"Well, you didn't even stay awake for your watch," said Glen bitterly. Then he made himself take a deep breath. All this arguing just wasted their energy anyway. "I'm going to try and work out how far it is still. But let's open those containers again. Thank goodness your mum insisted we had food."

"Thanks," said Alex awkwardly. "She does try her best."

Somehow the comment moved Glen. "I know she does," he muttered.

"I think we should take a look at the fire and see how near it's getting," said Alex.

Glen yawned. He felt as if he'd hardly slept at all. "How are we going to do that?" he asked.

"Have you ever thought of climbing a tree?" suggested Alex. "You know, those tall things with a trunk and branches…"

Alex swung himself stiffly up into a tall maple tree and Glen followed him, the thick branches easy to climb.

As they reached the top Glen gasped.

The fire seemed a lot nearer and the trees on the horizon weren't even visible in the pall of smoke which now hung over that part of the forest.

"How far?" asked Alex.

"A few miles away. Maybe six or seven," said Glen hopefully. But really he thought it was less.

"What are we going to do?"

They were standing on a topmost branch, staring out at the distant pall of smoke.

Glen was trying to work out what to do, knowing

that the time would come for them to take the risk of trying to scramble up the steep side of the falls. One false step and they would fall, and be swept away by the weight of the water. But what else could they do? The fire was getting closer – and even the smoke could kill them if they were to breathe too much of it in.

"So what do we do?" said Alex. "You got us into this, remember?"

"OK." Glen bit back his aggression. "I know it's all my fault." He felt a surge of relief. At least Alex must respect him more now – he was actually asking him what to do, relying on him as an equal, a companion. "It would be risky climbing up the falls," he said. "But if we can get back to the river we could try. We'd have to be really careful."

"It doesn't sound especially safe." Suddenly Alex grinned at Glen. "But if you reckon we can handle it—"

"There aren't too many other options."

But Glen was more concerned they'd never get back to the river and be lost in the forest for ever. And if this wasn't enough, even if they did make the river, they still had three potentially deadly enemies – the bears, the forest fire and the falls. But out of the three, the falls at least provided a possible escape route. They would have to try and climb them. They would have to take the initiative – and the terrible risk.

The Roaring River

Saturday, 7am

Having eaten some bread and cheese and a banana, with only one swig of water, Glen and Alex started out again, making their way through the forest using the map and with Alex calculating on his watch. Then, slowly, almost believing it must be an illusion, they saw the gleam of water through a break in the trees.

Glen was full of genuine gratitude to Alex.

"You're brilliant!" he said.

"What?" Alex sounded amazed at receiving a compliment from Glen.

"You're brilliant," he repeated. "That watch of yours really does help."

"And for my next trick," said Alex, for the first time light-hearted, "we're going to climb the falls!" He made the ascent sound easy, and Glen didn't want to disillusion him.

Alex and Glen came to a halt and gazed at the churning river. It was full of broken, blackened branches that had hurtled over the falls. The enormous mass of water was thundering out of the gorge, the spray rising as the shining river plunged down the rock face into boiling fury below.

Glen looked carefully at the rocky climb that was on their side of the falls. The rocks weren't sheer and he could see ledges and niches that they might be able to use. Maybe the climb was really possible after all.

"What are you like about heights?" Glen asked Alex.

"Not too good. But I can try." Alex looked anxiously at Glen. "You got any experience?"

"Yes. I've been on rock climbing courses with the school. If we both keep calm and are really careful we can make it." Glen's voice rang with what he thought was obvious false confidence.

"It's a risk," said Alex shakily. "Isn't it?"

"Sort of."

"We'll have to make it."

Glen nodded.

Alex was clasping and unclasping his hands, showing every sign of agitation. He was no longer the cool, laid-back figure who had shown such expertise in his kayak – although he had never been in one before. Alex was scared. But then so was Glen.

"If I go first," Glen said, "you can see where I put my feet and hands. Then do the same."

Lit by the morning sun, close up the falls were an even more devastating sight, a wall of water sparkling wickedly, as if it was grinning, daring them to try and climb the wet rock. The spray arched in a cold mist and Glen shuddered.

"You OK?" bellowed Alex. The roaring of the falls was now so loud that they could barely hear what the other was saying.

"You bet I am," yelled Glen, knowing he had to be

decisive. "We'll start climbing up." But still Glen hesitated. There were definite footholds, but the whole rockface seemed to be shifting, insubstantial in the mist, and Glen knew that they couldn't afford to misjudge one single step.

"Come on," said Alex impatiently. "Talk to me, Glen. Don't just stand there. Tell me what you know about climbing." There was a hint of shrillness in his voice and Glen was suddenly overcome with raw panic too, at the sound of Alex's fear. Somehow he managed to push it away, to get control, to reassure Alex.

"It's really straightforward. Watch me," Glen bawled. "Don't crouch down on the rock, however slippery it seems. Try and stand up and put your hands and feet where I put mine."

"Don't go too fast," Alex pleaded.

"I won't." Alex's anxiety seemed to be rising all the time. Will he be able to manage it? wondered Glen. "You were great at kayaking. You picked up the technique really fast. Now you can be a great rock climber too."

Alex shook his head, as if he couldn't imagine acquiring such an alien skill.

"OK," said Glen firmly. "Follow me."

Alex didn't reply, nor did he move.

"Follow me!" yelled Glen. "You'll be OK. I promise."

Finding a foothold immediately, Glen began to feel better. Having made a good start, he felt for another, and another. But Alex was level with him now, trying to get the ordeal over as quickly as he could.

Glen knew that this was a big mistake. "Stay back," he said. "I told you, follow me."

"I need to get up there," said Alex grimly. "I can't go at your pace. I've got to go at mine."

"Stay back."

"No way."

"It isn't as easy as you think."

"Why don't you shut up?"

Alex was overhauling him now, climbing over the slippery rock, getting hand and footholds where there seemed to be none. He was acting as if he had some sort of blind faith in himself.

Then the pain ripped right through Glen. "You idiot!" he shouted.

"What?"

"You trod on my hand."

"You should have moved faster—"

"I told you to follow me."

"I need to do my own thing," said Alex fiercely. "I don't want to hang about."

They climbed on up, wary of each other's presence on the rockface. There was a gust of strong wind and strands of smoke suddenly billowed over the falls, getting into their throats and nostrils and threatening to choke them.

"Are you OK?" yelled Glen above the roar of the water. He could see the strain on Alex's face and felt a short, sharp stab of terror, of over-reaching, of being about to make a deadly mistake. Again. But there was no alternative. They had to keep going.

A new and tense silence had now built up between them. For a terrible moment Glen looked down at the wall of water hitting the rocks below, sending up clouds of spray which were making the climb so much more difficult. For a split second he lost concentration. His foot slipped and for a ghastly moment Glen hung in space, the dreadful strain on his arms biting deep. Then he found a foothold and relief flooded through him, relief and elation and the most extraordinary primitive joy.

"Are you OK, Alex?" he bellowed.

"I'm OK," shouted Alex. But he didn't sound OK at all.

The rock surface had become even more slippery as they both arrived at a tricky section just below a larger ledge. Alex finally managed to pull himself on to the ledge, then carried on up. When Glen reached it he paused, revelling in the temporary feeling of safety. Maybe the climb *was* going to be manageable, he thought.

Then Glen looked up at Alex – and saw that he had frozen to the rocky surface and was blocking his way.

Alex was clinging to the rock, shaking violently and giving little whimpers of pain and terror.

"What's the matter?"

"I'm stuck." Alex's voice was high with panic.

"There's a crevice just above your right foot."

"Where?"

"Feel for it." Glen watched Alex's foot flail around. "Slowly and carefully feel for it."

"I'm going to fall." Alex's panic was increasing.

"No you're not." Glen forced himself to sound calm.

"I can't find anywhere to put my foot." Alex gave a half sob. Then there was a roaring sound, a roaring that was very different from the noise of the falls. Alex looked down for a moment and so did Glen. Then Alex began to scream.

The male grizzly was enormous, peering up at them from the rocky path at the bottom of the falls. Now he was making a lower growling sound, as if warning Glen and Alex that they were trespassing on his territory. But a bear couldn't climb the falls, could it? Of course it couldn't, Glen reasoned to himself.

"Just ignore him," Glen said sharply, acutely aware of how banal he must sound. "He can't get at us."

"He's willing me to fall."

"Don't be stupid," yelled Glen. "Now I told you – there's a crevice above your foot. Move."

"I can't hold on any longer."

"Of course you can. Lift your right foot." Glen's voice was sharp.

"Where?"

"Straight up. Feel for it."

"I can't."

The grizzly's growling increased gradually until he was making a deep roaring sound again. His bellowing merged with the thunder of the falls, both sounds seemed to batter against the boys, compelling them to fall.

"Get on with it!" yelled Glen.

"I can't move."

"Just – lift – your – right – foot!" shouted Glen.

But Alex didn't seem to hear. He was clinging to the rock, his body wracked by violent spasms of shivering. Glen was climbing alongside him now, slowly but steadily.

"Watch where I put my feet," he said. "Just do what I do."

But as he glanced back at Alex and saw how pale he was, Glen suddenly felt deeply afraid, more afraid than he had ever felt in his life before. His mouth was dry and his heart was hammering painfully, beads of cold sweat breaking out on his forehead. He had to get through to Alex!

"Move it, Alex!" Glen yelled desperately, not knowing what to do to galvanize him into action, the fear making his own grip less certain by the second. "Do it! Just *do* it!"

At the bottom of the falls the bear roared again and suddenly Alex was climbing. For a moment Glen was relieved, then he saw that Alex wasn't trying to follow him, but was branching out on his own. The more the bear roared, the harder and faster Alex climbed.

"Slow down!" Glen shouted, sure that if Alex didn't slow down he'd come off the rockface and fall into the river below. He'd never survive that. He wouldn't stand a chance. Nausea swept through Glen. In desperation he felt for the next foothold and began to pull himself up.

Now both of them were climbing parallel to each other, more slowly, but deftly and without hesitation. Then when the bear roared again Alex began to climb faster once more, outstripping Glen and straining for the top.

"Be careful!" shouted Glen. "Slow *down*!"

But Alex had reached the top and was hauling himself over. He disappeared momentarily and then reappeared again, standing up and yelling at Glen.

"I made it!"

Glen was with him in a few moments, also hauling himself safely over to stand shakily at the top of the falls.

Alex grabbed his arm and Glen felt a great elation spreading inside him.

They'd made it! They'd made it together!

Alex and Glen gazed down at the vast wall of water. The bear had disappeared.

"I couldn't have done it without you," gasped Alex.

"You couldn't have done it without the bear," retorted Glen with a smile.

"I'm going to take a break," said Alex and he lay down on the rocky bank of the river, trying to make himself comfortable.

"We'd better not go to sleep though," Glen said. "This is still bear country."

Alex grinned at him. "How could I have forgotten?"

Then Glen sat down. "But we can risk a sit down," he said. "We deserve a rest."

They gazed at the hurtling river as it plunged over the falls and into the gorge. The misty spray dampened their faces and the roaring sound was relentless, making their heads ache. But it was still much less forbidding than the roaring of the bear.

"You know," said Alex, "in all modesty, we haven't done that badly getting up here."

"I did very badly by getting you into this situation in the first place," said Glen miserably. "And Dad's going to kill me when we get back."

"I'll stick up for you," said Alex unexpectedly, and Glen looked at him gratefully. He had expected Alex to curse him for bringing the subject up again. Had a bond been built between them? he wondered.

"Will you really?"

"Yes."

"But I made such a—"

"Shut up!" snapped Alex this time. "Just shut up. We're getting on OK, aren't we?"

"Yes," said Glen. "I suppose we are."

Fire Moves Fast

Saturday, 11am

Feeling totally exhausted, Glen and Alex still sat by the river's edge. And then, the acrid smell of fire began to fill their nostrils again.

"We've got to move on," said Glen. "We can't stay here."

"Where're we going?"

"I don't know! We should keep following the river's direction if possible but I'm not even sure which way the fire's coming from with all this smoke."

"What should we do then?"

Glen realised that Alex was dependent on him

again. It seemed that when threatened Alex relied on his own survival tactics, but when a decision had to be made he was beginning to rely on Glen.

"Well, there's too much undergrowth to walk along the river's edge here. We'll have to go back in to the trees and hope the fire is still far enough away," said Glen. "Let's use your watch compass again."

Alex looked down at his watch and made some calculations. "This way," he said. "It's your turn to follow me."

Dazed, still utterly exhausted and not thinking straight, the boys got up and began to walk into the gathering darkness of the trees. The smoke's getting thicker, thought Glen. Soon we won't be able to see where we're going. And he realised that this part of the forest would, at some point, be torched by the encroaching fire and felt sick with apprehension and terror.

As Alex and Glen trudged on, they were increasingly aware of the fire coming closer, and eventually the smoke became so thick that they had to pull off their sweatshirts and wind them round their mouths and noses.

We'll never make it, thought Glen, as the noise of the burning became louder. He pulled off his improvised mask and yelled at Alex who was a few metres in front. "The fire's getting worse."

Alex increased his speed and as Glen raced after him he saw that the trees were becoming more spread out, with groups of oaks and even the occasional clearing. He felt that this should mean something to him, but he was so tired and smoky he couldn't work out what.

Then Glen had a moment of clarity. What on earth were they doing? They seemed to be speeding *towards* the fire. Making a furious effort, he caught up with Alex, grabbed his shoulder and swung him round.

"What is it?" Alex gasped, taking his jumper from his face.

"We're running into the fire. We've got to get back to the river and take our chances back there. Maybe we'll have to wade in. This is crazy!"

"The current's too strong to wade in the river. We'll be washed back over the falls. We have to keep going, get back—"

Suddenly, there was a grunting sound and to their horror they saw a bear cub, half hidden in a thicket of brambles around the base of an oak tree.

Alex and Glen looked around fearfully, but there was no immediate sign of the mother, although the smoke was gradually obscuring everything. The cub was making choking noises and was obviously in distress.

"We have to help the cub," Glen managed to gasp out.

"What do you suggest?" said Alex sarcastically. "Giving him a piggyback? Are you losing your mind?"

Still Glen hesitated.

"Are you insane?" yelled Alex.

"Where's the mother?"

"I don't want to wait and find out!"

Now the smoke was even thicker and they were starting to have trouble breathing themselves.

Then, as if at some silent signal, the cub turned away and began to run – although the smoke made it impossible to tell where it had gone.

"Come on!" yelled Alex. He pushed on again, checking his watch, as Glen still stood there, wondering if the cub had finally sensed his mother's whereabouts. If only I had a mother I could run to who'd keep me safe, Glen thought as he stumbled after Alex, pushing his stiffening legs to the limit.

Then, quite suddenly, they found themselves in a large smoke-laden clearing. Glen paused, looking round wildly. The smoke was making him dizzy but the clearing reminded him of something again. What was it? Then it came to him. "If we move fast we could make a firebreak," he said.

"How?" Alex was doubtful.

"I read about it somewhere." Glen suddenly sounded inspired. "You burn a circle of grass and bushes right down to the ground and then lie down inside the circle. The fire should sweep right over you."

Alex didn't reply.

Glen dragged off his rucksack and started to rummage for the matches – which he couldn't immediately find.

After a while Alex couldn't be patient any longer. "The fire's almost on us," he shouted. His face was flushed with heat and exertion. But Glen had found the matches at last and was bending over the long dry grass at the edge of the clearing, lighting match after match as he walked round in a circle. The dry grass caught at once and began to burn. Glen looked up at the main fire. He thought it was only about half a kilometre away now.

The grass and small bushes in the middle of the clearing blazed fiercely and Glen and Alex watched them anxiously. But to their intense relief the flames had nothing to feed on after a while and went out.

"We have to lie down there?" asked Alex, and Glen could see he was regretting the whole idea. He hesitated, looking at the circle of burnt grass. Then they both saw the fire roaring towards them, an orange wall of flame, while ash started to fall on them like rain. It was an awesome sight.

But before Glen and Alex could move, a chattering sound exploded overhead and through the billowing smoke they saw a couple of helicopters, hovering low.

"Shout at them!" yelled Glen. "Wave your arms!"

Alex and Glen began to jump up and down on the spot, shouting and yelling, waving their arms. But as the smoke thickened, the helicopters began to fly higher until they disappeared completely.

"They can't have seen us," said Glen, feeling like

giving up. Maybe if they just lay down and closed their eyes the smoke would take them. And if the smoke didn't, the flames soon would. He had never felt so drained and exhausted in his life.

"They wouldn't have been able to land in all this smoke. But I think they *did* see us." Alex was trying to reassure Glen now.

"They did?" Glen felt a tiny spark of hope. Then it died. Even if they *had* spotted them, the helicopters had gone, the fire was almost on them and they were alone. He gazed down at their own burnt out patch. It seemed ludicrous to think it could give them shelter. Why *should* the fire leap? They were going to burn to death.

"This *is* going to work, Glen. It's a good idea," Alex shouted above the noise of the approaching fire. He lay down on his front, with his jumper over his mouth again, pulling Glen down beside him.

They waited, listening to the sound of the blaze, all too aware of its rapid progress. Then Glen looked up and saw elk and deer running a little ahead of the flames, while white eagles and hawks flew high over the fire, hovering, knowing that their prey would soon be flushed out.

Then dimly, through the smoke and fire, Alex saw a blurred, but all too familiar shape. He choked and coughed, but still couldn't drag his eyes away. The heavy bodies, the deadly paws, the—

"Watch out!" shouted Alex. "Grizzlies!"

There must have been half a dozen of them with their cubs, pounding past the boys and away from danger at tremendous speed, disappearing into the darkness of the trees, only just ahead of the leaping fire.

Then Glen cried out in terror and Alex stared in silence as the great red mass of flame hurtled towards them, a burning wall in direct contrast to the wall of water they had just survived.

"OK," said Alex, quietly and steadily. "Time to test out the firebreak." He lay down on his stomach, pressing himself into the earth. Glen did the same, wriggling into the ground as much as he could, hearing the blaze that was crackling around them and occasionally roaring like the wildest of wild animals. Then he felt his clothes scorching in the searing heat and assumed the worst. The flames weren't going to jump them. The heat was incredible, suffocating, too much to bear. Glen knew they were going to burn. Soon his smouldering clothes would burst into flames.

Suddenly the ferocity of the heat went away and there was a whooshing sound. Cautiously, Glen turned over on his back and saw that the wall of fire was in the trees behind them. But there was still a good deal of swirling smoke that was making him choke and retch. He couldn't even see Alex, it was so thick. Slowly, very slowly, the air cleared slightly, but Glen went on coughing. And what about Alex? Glen couldn't hear him coughing, was he OK? At last the dim shape of Alex lying on the ground next to him became clear. Glen could just make out a smile on Alex's grimy face and he grinned back in relief. Alex was still here, still alive. He hadn't left him like… Maybe they would be OK.

"It went over us," croaked Alex. "We did it. You were right. The fire jumped the gap!"

Glen smiled back at him, but as the smoke continued to clear he suddenly saw more flames approaching them from the right this time, and not that far away. "No!" he yelled and Alex sat up in alarm.

To his horror Glen could see a second front of fire – perhaps three quarters of a kilometre away, but already sending out sparks and a hail of debris.

"I can't take any more of this!" Alex began to struggle to his feet.

"We have to stay together!" shouted Glen.

"Make for the river!" Alex was already up and running and Glen knew he had to follow. Why hadn't they stayed near the water in the first place? he wondered. Surely the river was the best kind of firebreak possible? OK, so they couldn't walk along it because of the undergrowth, but they could have got in it, in the shallows. Still he couldn't force his legs to move as the second front of the burning forest leapt towards them.

Then he was aware of Alex's hand on his shoulder and felt a surge of confidence. At least he could trust Alex. He'd come back for him.

"For God's sake," Glen heard Alex shouting. "What's the matter with you?"

"Nothing," mumbled Glen.

"Then start moving. Unless you really want to be burnt to a crisp."

They ran, side by side, until the trees came closer and they were in single file, Alex in the lead, Glen a few paces behind.

The crackling sound was still all around them and the smell of burning began to mix with the smoke, leaving an acrid taste in their throats once again. Glen and Alex, their sweatshirts still being used as inadequate masks, continued to sprint through the trees.

Branches fell a few metres away, a mass of flame. When Glen looked round he saw the treetops themselves were burning, and some of the pines and oaks were beginning to topple, the sky above them still darkened by smoke and flame.

"Don't go that way!" yelled Glen as Alex began to head towards the river at an angle Glen was sure was wrong.

Alex came to a halt, gasping for breath. "What are you on about?" he bellowed.

"You're going too far downriver. That'll take us back to the falls! We'll be trapped. Our only chance is to get higher upriver, further from the falls, and try to see if we can make it across to the other bank. Otherwise, the fire will catch up with us!" Glen began to cough again.

Alex grabbed angrily at Glen's arm. "You're always so sure you're right. Well, you're not! What about taking us over the rapids? What about—"

Glen shook him off and Alex reeled back.

For a moment they gazed at each other, the old hostility briefly returning. Then Alex mumbled, "I shouldn't have said that. I was as stupid about that mother bear as you were about the rapids."

"No, you weren't as bad as me," insisted Glen. "Nowhere near as bad."

Suddenly Alex began to laugh. "Are we really quarrelling about who's taken the prize for stupidity?" he wailed, the sound so infectious that Glen soon joined in, their laughter increasing, slightly hysterical, as they gazed at each other's blood-streaked faces and the torn and stinking sweatshirts they were using as masks.

But in the silence that followed they could still hear the crackling of the advancing fire.

"Come on," said Glen. "We've got to get across the river somehow." But they still didn't know how to get further upriver – how to reach the river at all – and Glen knew that Alex would have no time to work miracles with his watch.

Alex looked up as a huge pine began to fall, bringing down another. They hit the forest floor about half a kilometre away from the boys, a mass of flame and smoke and sparks.

Glen lurched into a stumbling run and Alex followed closely behind him. It was then that they saw the grizzly.

"Stay still," whispered Glen, and this time Alex stayed where he was despite the fact that he was shaking all over. So was Glen.

But the grizzly hurtled along, followed by another, both heading in the same direction, ignoring them completely, intent only on escaping the deadly heat.

"We'll follow them!" yelled Glen, as the bears wheeled to the right.

"What?"

"Follow the bears. They know the forest. They must be looking for safety and they know where they're going – it must be to the river."

Glen pounded after the grizzlies, just managing to keep them in sight.

"We've got to keep going!" he bellowed at Alex. "If we lose them, we're done for!"

But inwardly Glen was in despair. They were both utterly exhausted and choking so badly that they couldn't possibly keep up with the bears' pace. Then Glen saw the familiar glint of water, and by a miracle they'd definitely come out further upriver. He shouted with wild joy, whirling his charred sweatshirt above his head and tearing off his rucksack. He ran to the tree-hung bank and threw himself into the shallows at the edge of the river.

The grizzlies were nowhere to be seen.

Alex followed him in, pulling off his own rucksack, and they rolled about in the shallow water, shouting in exultation, letting the coolness soothe their aching bodies.

Then Glen began to drink, forgetting about the bacteria.

"Don't!" Alex shouted at him.

"Why not?"

"The river's full of bugs – remember? I told you before."

"Too bad. I'll take the risk." Glen knelt down and

ducked his head and drank again while Alex stood watching him for a moment and then knelt down and drank too, gulping the water down as fast as he could.

When their thirsts were quenched they looked back to see that parts of the wooded bank behind them were now ablaze and sparks were hitting the surface of the water. Occasionally a burning tree on the bank fell in a great shower of steam.

Despite the fact that the water in the shallows was slow-moving, the centre of the river was still flowing swiftly, whirling cindery tree trunks and branches downstream. There was even a whole tree that had virtually been reduced to charcoal.

"We've got to get across," said Alex, gazing at the opposite bank that seemed like a paradise of tranquillity, with cool dark trees hanging over the water.

"We'd never get across here without being taken downstream again. The current's too strong," said Glen. "Got any other ideas?" There was a desperate pleading in his tone.

Alex looked longingly at the opposite bank and then gazed intently at the river.

"Don't even think about it," said Glen. "Don't even think about trying to swim across. It may be shallow here, but the current's really strong in the middle."

"What about further up?"

"Maybe. I reckon all we can do is walk along in the shallows of the river and see if we can find a place to cross upstream."

"How long is *that* going to take us?"

"Impossible to say," said Glen bleakly.

"What are they going to think? Your dad. My mum. They won't have the faintest idea where we are," said Alex.

"I know that."

"Or will your father have guessed—" Alex broke off.

"That I was stupid enough to try and wind you up?" Glen looked away. "To slip under the chain?"

"Will he?" said Alex quietly.

"I'm not sure. He'd have hoped I wouldn't. But then—"

"He might have sussed you out?"

"He might," said Glen uneasily. "I hope he has." He paused. "But maybe he'll think I was too sensible."

"I hope not," said Alex fervently.

"So do I." Glen suddenly grinned. "I'm sorry, Alex."

"Don't keep saying that."

"Why not?"

"It gets on my nerves!" But Alex grinned back at him.

"And mine," said Glen. "Let's get going."

Stiffly they struggled to their feet and began to stumble on in the shallows of the river, sparks from the fire shooting over their heads. Soon, however, to his fearful relief, Glen saw that they seemed to be leaving the flames behind, but not the smoke which was drifting in great swathes across the river. The bank had broadened out again and was no longer ablaze so they were able to walk along together, their throats sore, wheezing slightly and carrying the depressing knowledge that they still had no chance of crossing.

Glen and Alex walked on for another half hour, their breathing laboured and heads spinning but some of their stiffness easing. Eventually they were both so exhausted that, for a few minutes, they lay down for a rest.

*

When Glen woke, he immediately panicked, aware that they had once again fallen asleep and lost a lot of time. The temperature was cooler and the sun was much lower in the sky. He reckoned they might only have a couple of hours of daylight left.

"How long did we sleep for?" Alex was sitting up and staring glassily ahead of him, then looking at his watch.

But Glen wasn't listening. "Look at that!"

In their exhaustion they'd barely noticed that the river had got narrower and the opposite bank was nearer. For a moment their spirits lifted, but then they saw that a bridge of fire was spanning this narrower reach. A tall tree had fallen and was resting on the opposite bank, forming a blazing arch.

"What are we going to do?" demanded Glen helplessly, not wanting Alex to rely on him.

"I don't know." Alex's voice was almost a whisper.

"We'll have to try to get across." Glen was forming yet another desperate idea that might – just might – work. "It's still our only hope. OK, so that tree's on fire, but the flames haven't reached the other bank. If we get a move on we might be able to keep in front of it."

Alex's mind was also racing ahead. "If we dive deep, we should be able to swim under that arch of fire and get further up the bank."

Glen realised that Alex was right. If they managed to swim under the arch, they could land further up, and unless the wind changed, the bank higher up should still be clear of the fire. He was deeply grateful to Alex, although Glen couldn't think why he hadn't had the idea himself. It seemed so simple now.

"The current will push us back though," Alex said miserably, having second thoughts.

"Not if we fight like crazy!"

"I've got no fight left in me."

"Yes you have," said Glen firmly. "We can't give up now. What kind of swimmer are you?"

"*Now* you ask me." Alex was silent. Then he said cautiously, "I used to be OK. But I haven't swum for years. Not since Dad left."

"We're going to have to fight the current, but the river's so much narrower we've definitely got a chance."

"Is this the last problem we've got?" asked Alex.

"Or are there going to be more later?"

"Don't think ahead. Let's just get our act together now," Glen insisted. "I'm going to give a count to three. Then we go, one after the other. Got it?"

"Got it," said Alex. "But there's one thing we've forgotten."

"What?"

"The rucksacks. We'll have to abandon them, and that means all our food and water as well. But you just can't swim underwater with a rucksack. Not unless you're some kind of stuntman."

"OK," said Glen, taking his rucksack off his back and dumping it on the bank. "One – two – three—"

Glen dived.

After a slight hesitation, Alex followed.

Glen struggled, feeling the force of the current, swimming underwater as hard as he could, encouraged by the thought that he was making progress in the shadowy depths. How far had he got to go now? His lungs were beginning to hurt, but if he surfaced now he could come up right under the blazing arch.

Opening his eyes, he glanced behind him and saw

Alex's dim shape, but immediately lost momentum and wished he hadn't.

Glen began to battle forward again; his lungs were hurting badly now. A wave of panic swept over him. Again he wondered how far away the arch of fire was. Would he be able to judge when he had cleared it? He quickened his stroke, trying to make more headway, but the more he panicked, the less progress he seemed to make, and for a moment Glen wondered if he was actually swimming on the spot.

Feeling as if his lungs were about to burst, Glen broke the surface to sudden heat. He immediately realised he still hadn't cleared the arch and took an enormous breath, diving down before the heat of the flames could scorch his head.

This time Glen tried to swim harder and faster, and although the pressure in his lungs soon began to build up all over again, he was determined not to surface. He thrashed on, closing his eyes, lungs bursting.

Eventually he surfaced again, gasping in triumph as he saw that the burning tree that spanned the river was a few metres behind him. Remaining on the surface Glen swam on, cleaving the water, determinedly propelling himself into the shallows.

Buoyed up by the achievement of having cleared the arch, Glen managed to reach the far bank. He grabbed at a tree root, pulled himself out and turned to look desperately out across the water for Alex.

Then he saw him surface, spluttering, a wide grin of delight spreading across his face as he, too, realised he had outstripped the arch of fire.

"Glen!" he yelled.

"What is it?"

"Thanks!"

"What for?"

"Not letting me give up!"

As Alex dragged himself out, their eyes met and Glen could really feel the bond between them.

"Wait a minute," Glen said, looking around him.

"What is it?"

"We're *not* on the opposite bank at all!" Glen could hardly believe they'd been given such luck after so many difficulties. "We're on an island – and so far the fire *hasn't* spread to the other bank, or the island. It's like a miracle!"

Alex was elated. "We've really got a chance

now – maybe for the first time we've really got a chance!" Then he grabbed Glen's hand and shook it fiercely. "We're partners now!" he exclaimed. "Real partners!"

Glen closed his eyes against the tears of happiness.

Battle for the Territory

Saturday, 6pm

Twilight was deepening the shadows. Cautiously, Glen and Alex decided to check the far side of the island for the best place to cross the river. But when Glen looked up he saw the sky was black. Could there be a storm on the way?

Let the clouds burst, he thought; if people couldn't put out the fire, then maybe the heavens might.

"Do you think it's going to rain?" asked Alex, but Glen didn't want to commit himself.

"Maybe. Impossible to tell whether it's smoke, or a

storm coming."

"If we do have a storm, the rain *could* put the fire out, couldn't it?" Alex was hesitant.

"We'd have to have a torrential downpour to do that."

"Let's wait," said Alex.

"What for?"

"The storm, you idiot."

"It might not come for ages. The storm might not come at all."

Glen realised they were on the brink of quarrelling again. "We have to push on," he persisted, expecting Alex to contradict him, and relieved when he didn't. But now, even if they argued, they did seem to be able to work it out. "We need to find a place where we can jump to the other side," Glen continued. "Or maybe swim again if the current's not too fierce."

They walked slowly and warily through the trees, soon reaching the far side. Here the island had broadened out a little and the channel was narrower. But it was still too wide to jump and very fast flowing.

Despondently they continued to walk upriver, keeping a sharp look-out for a better place to cross.

Slowly the trees thinned, to be replaced by bushes and long, waist-high grass.

"Wait! I thought I heard something," Alex said suddenly. Slowly, they both began to edge forwards until they could see flattened long grass ahead of them.

Glen's heart gave a lurch that was sudden and painful. The rank smell was there, deep and oppressive. Had they – could they have – arrived on enemy territory?

"Don't move," said Glen.

"What's happening?"

"Stand still."

Alex gave a gasp. "You only say that when—" Alex couldn't finish his sentence, but Glen knew he had to finish it for him.

"When grizzlies are around."

"Not again!" groaned Alex, shivering in his wet clothes.

Glen supposed it was the fire which had forced the bears to arrive in one place. Their territories were huge and normally the grizzlies never moved in groups.

Alex was gazing ahead, listening intently.

"Where are they?" whispered Glen, wanting to relinquish any spark of leadership or initiative. They'd been through so much. Hadn't the wild finished with them yet? Or had it been waiting to kill them all the time?

Alex was moving forward again, beckoning to Glen to follow, until they reached another clump of trees and peered out cautiously, seeing more flattened grass around them. The trees had been deeply scratched and coarse black hairs were caught in the bark.

Then they both heard the grunting – and froze.

Before they could reach another clump of trees they saw the two male grizzlies rise up from the grass to lock with each other in mortal combat, roaring fiercely – just as fiercely as the falls and the flames of the forest fire.

Glen felt a rush of ice cold fear churning in his stomach. We managed to climb the falls, he thought, we managed to escape flames. But are the hungry, frightened, hostile grizzlies going to get us at the final moment – after we've at last finished trying to battle each other to death?

Glen was reminded of boxers in a ring, but there were no rules here, there was no referee. Glen knew he was about to watch a fight to the death. This was the animal kingdom where everything was part of the pecking order – as were they.

One of the bears was bigger than the other, but his smaller opponent seemed to fight the hardest. Glen and Alex watched in horrified fascination as the bears lunged at each other, making painful contact, trading blow for blow, roaring in frustration and anger.

"Who are you rooting for?" whispered Alex.

"The small one," replied Glen, and immediately felt ashamed. Both bears were standing up on their hind legs now, using their huge paws against each other, as well as their claws. Soon bright red blood was running down their fur and a great slash mark appeared on the larger bear's shoulder.

The grizzlies made grunting sounds as they fought and gradually Glen became sickened by their aggression. Yet he and Alex could have behaved like this. Thank God they hadn't gone this far, he thought. Thank God they had avoided the final battle. The bonding had taken over. He glanced at Alex, seeing his rigid face muscles and the horror of it all reflected in his eyes. Glen could sense that Alex was thinking much the same as he was.

Then the larger bear, now on all fours, charged at his opponent, clawing at his flank, while the smaller bear bit back, fastening its huge jaws and sharp teeth into his rival's shoulder. Their two heads remained buried in each other's fur until with a violent shake the smaller bear pulled away, leaving another huge gash in his opponent's shoulder.

For a moment they backed off and stood still, waiting for the right moment to spring again.

They were still grunting, breathing heavily, their eyes locked. Blood from the gashes on the larger bear's shoulders was streaming to the ground in a bright red flow.

"I think he's had it," whispered Alex.

"We shouldn't be watching."

Glen looked at what he imagined was hatred in the bear's eyes and remembered all the hatred he had had for Alex and the terrible risk he had taken to humiliate him. Now he no longer felt the hatred and he didn't want to be reminded of it. But these were grizzlies. They only had instincts. They couldn't reason with each other.

The roaring began again as both bears leapt, forcing

each other to the ground, rolling over, biting at each other. The terrible fight seemed to continue for a very long time. Then, slowly, the smaller bear got on top. He ripped at the throat of his opponent and as more blood fountained up, the bigger bear's roaring became a howl of pain.

Now the larger bear lay still on the flattened grass, making a wheezing sound that was horrible to hear. But the smaller bear didn't back off, continuing to slash and hammer at him.

Glen saw that the eyes of the wounded bear were beginning to cloud over. His body continued to twitch, but eventually he lay still while the victor stood over his opponent for a while before he finally lumbered away.

In the sudden stillness, the dead bear twitched slightly again and Alex moved forward.

"Where are you going?" Glen hissed.

Alex didn't reply and Glen hurried to catch him up as he began to stumble over to the enormous black hump in the grass. Glen felt he was being drawn towards the grizzly against his will, against all his new-found survival instincts, dragged on by Alex's need to get closer.

Did Alex really want to look at the spoils of the victor,

to gaze down at the dead bear? This was violence in the wild. But this was how humans could also end up if they gave way to their primitive instincts, thought Glen, glancing across at Alex. Had he been drawn to the dying bear for the same reason? he wondered. To see the self-destruction they'd both avoided.

The two boys stood respectfully beside the grizzly which looked bloody and massive and tragic, all at the same time. The broad strong head with its open mouth, showing the huge teeth, had an air of vulnerability. In death, the bear had a dignity that was unexpectedly moving.

They stood without speaking, Glen remembering his mother, wondering again if his father blamed him for her death. Now he had been out in the wild, he felt he'd been wrong about that. Glen was beginning to realise that sometimes terrible things happened, in nature too, and that the terrible thing wasn't necessarily anyone's fault. Sometimes animals died – sometimes they survived.

Alex also seemed to be a long way off. Then he said abruptly, "I was thinking about my father. He left a long time ago. We never see him now. It's as if he's dead."

"Like my mother."

"I'm sorry – I didn't mean—" Alex looked at him in sudden distress. "I didn't mean to be—"

"I know you didn't," said Glen. "It's OK. At least I can talk about her now." Then his mood changed. "We'd better get going. We'd still be safer if we could find some way across the river."

"Right," agreed Alex, but neither of them moved for a while as they stood, heads bowed, over the massive corpse as if they were mourners at a funeral.

Then slowly, and uneasily, Glen remembered something. "Where's the other grizzly gone?"

Alex gasped.

They had both forgotten the surviving bear's existence as they stood over the corpse. The boys gazed around them, but there was no sign of the grizzly in the long grass beyond the area of the fight. That didn't mean he wasn't around though, Glen realised, watching them, stalking them, probably desperately hungry.

Glen and Alex walked warily back through the long grass, eventually finding a place which broadened out still further where the gap between the island and the other bank of the river was quite narrow.

Alex nodded confidently. "I reckon I could jump that," he said.

"Only with a grizzly behind you," muttered Glen. As he looked down into the dark, churning water he wondered how he was ever going to get off the island. He'd never be able to jump the gap. He wondered why Alex was so confident. They had come through so much that he must just think he could survive anything! The gap was well over two metres wide.

"We'll be taken downriver again if we fall in," Glen pointed out. "And because the channel's narrow, the water's running really fast." He stared down again at the churning torrent which was twisting and turning in a series of small whirlpools.

"We *could* get sucked down in that lot," Alex agreed. Then he seemed to pull himself together, to be more resolute. "But we just need to take a very long run up and not think too hard about the gap."

"You reckon that's possible?" Glen was doubtful.

"We can't stay here." Alex's voice shook. "That grizzly must still be around. Maybe he's nursing his wounds, but he won't be doing that for long."

Glen knew that Alex was right. "We'll have to jump," he said, looking at Alex's long legs with envy. "I suppose that was your big advantage at school. Your most successful sport. The long jump."

"How did you guess?"

"I tend to notice other people's height, being rather on the short side myself." Glen tried to make a joke about the problem.

Alex thought for a moment. Then he turned to Glen. "We'll jump together. You'll be OK."

As Alex started to back away, Glen suddenly noticed that the long grass was stirring. For what seemed a very long while he continued to watch the stirring, unable to speak, just as he'd been unable to speak when Kate was about to fall. But that episode seemed light years away. Then Glen hissed, "Something's coming."

"What?" Alex seemed distracted as he gazed measuringly at the opposite bank. Then he suddenly seemed to realise what Glen had said. "What are you on about?"

"Keep still!" Glen whispered. "There's a grizzly behind you."

Alex gazed at Glen in disbelief. "How *can* you send me up at a time like this?"

"I'm not. For God's sake, Alex, don't move. Stay where you are."

But Alex was already racing towards the riverbank as the grizzly broke cover. Running as fast as he could, Alex jumped the gap between the island and the far bank, just making the other side. But the bear wasn't pursuing him.

Motionless with fright, Glen darted a glance behind him and was relieved to see the grizzly was moving away, more frightened of their presence than they were of him.

But Glen had never felt so isolated. He should have run with Alex and leapt the gap, but he was still standing here, paralysed with shock.

"Run!" yelled Alex. "Run!" He was shouting out the word over and over again, bawling at the top of his voice. Glen knew Alex was rooting for him, but the gap seemed enormous and he was sure he would fall into the river.

Then, somehow, his mind seemed to force his legs to run; slowly and stiffly he pushed himself towards the bank and, without thinking whether he would make it or not, launched himself into space.

As he had expected, Glen fell just short of the bank. Plunging into the fast-running current, he was hurled along and a sense of utter defeat seized him.

"There's a branch," a voice shouted.

In the cold, cold water Glen was beginning to feel numb, to want to give up and slide under the surface of the river. But the voice wouldn't stop yelling at him.

"Grab the branch!"

Glen looked up and saw that a tree was hanging over the river with a strong branch trailing into the water.

"*Now!*" the voice yelled again. "Grab the branch now!"

Somewhere in the distance Glen could hear the voice, still shouting at him, using words he couldn't make out. But he had grabbed at the branch, as he had been told to, and when the panic receded he was surprised to see Alex was actually lying in the grass on the bank above him, his legs clamped round the trunk of a tree, shouting instructions.

"Grab my wrists," he was yelling. "I'll pull you in."

Glen clutched at Alex's wrists and hung on tightly as he was dragged up on to the bank. He felt child-like, dependent – as if Alex was much older.

As he landed in the long grass, Glen looked up at Alex. "Thanks," he said. "You've saved my life." He found he was trembling now, the shock coursing through him.

"You'd have done the same," said Alex. "You already have really – the climb, remember. And you could have made that jump. You just didn't believe in yourself enough."

Glen nodded. "At least we got away from that bear," he said. "He was already clawing at me in my mind."

"We have to check out this side of the river," said Alex. "The fire could have travelled over the tree from that island and set light to the grass here."

"No," replied Glen, trying to recover. "It hasn't done that. You can see for yourself."

"Are we safe?" demanded Alex.

"I think so."

Alex was beginning to tremble himself now. "That's not good enough!" he yelled, suddenly losing control. "That's not good enough at all. I need to be safe!"

"We are safe," said Glen. "You can rely on me."

Alex suddenly grinned at him and mock punched his shoulder. "Do you know, I believe I can."

For some moments, they stayed where they were, silent and unable to move, too exhausted to make any more decisions.

Then they heard a buzzing sound coming from somewhere upriver.

Alex grabbed Glen's arm, dragging him along the bank.

"Come on!" he shouted. "There's a boat!"

But Glen was now so tired he couldn't seem to make the connection.

"For God's sake!" Alex tightened his grip on Glen's arm. "You've *got* to run. We'll miss the boat if we don't hurry."

"So what?" Missing a boat meant nothing to Glen in his present state.

But Alex was becoming frantic. "They've seen us!"

he shouted. "Come on, Glen. Move, for God's sake. *Move!*"

Glen was finally stumbling ahead, heart hammering, racing for the riverbank, seeing the motorboat being moored to a tree, with a ranger just about to disembark. He could hardly believe what he was watching. People had come. At last the wilderness was inhabited. Then Glen told himself, we're people, Alex and I. But just for the moment Glen felt like a wild animal.

As Alex and Glen, panting and gasping, reached the ranger, he came forward to meet them and bustled them into the boat. "You survived! It's incredible! How did you do it?"

Glen said nothing. He didn't know what to say.

But Alex did. "We had an accident," he said firmly. "So we *had* to survive, didn't we? Sometimes we didn't think we were going to – but we worked on it together."

Not all the time, thought Glen.

"Where were you kayaking?" asked the ranger quietly as he handed them blankets, and Glen turned away. He could hardly believe they were safe, but now they were, the moment he had been dreading had come.

Glen knew he was going to be blamed – and rightly so. But he was so weak, so exhausted, he couldn't handle it.

"We were on the river," said Alex. "In the white water."

Glen tried to find words but once again he couldn't.

"Didn't you see the warning signs?"

"We made a mistake," said Alex.

The ranger nodded. "You ought to see yourselves," he said. "You look like—"

"Animals?" Glen found his voice at last. "Wild animals."

"Not exactly," laughed the ranger. "But getting close. You did brilliantly to survive, but I can't understand why you—"

"How did you track us down?" asked Alex hurriedly, and Glen realised that Alex was determined to protect him.

"We've been looking for you two since Friday evening. Then the helicopter saw the firebreak you'd made. You've been incredibly resourceful."

"Glen thought of the firebreak," said Alex.

"Wait a minute," began Glen. "I have to tell you that this is all my fault."

"Shut up," said Alex. "Don't listen to him," he advised the ranger.

The ranger looked thoughtfully from Glen to Alex. "Don't talk now," he said, seeing how drained and exhausted they both were. "You're too tired. And to survive out here – especially with the fire – I mean that's a real miracle. However you ended up here in the first place." He was looking at both of them with considerable respect as he started the boat once more.

A warm glow filled Glen and when he looked at Alex he winked at him. The bonding was deeper. Much deeper.

As the boat sped back up the river, Glen and Alex could see that most of the pines had fallen and there were only burnt stumps and layers of grey ash. But occasionally they could pick out a gaunt and smoke-blackened sentinel pine that had just escaped the fire.

Then Glen saw a mother grizzly pounding through the debris, her cub just behind her, trustingly following, and suddenly realised that he didn't feel as distressed about his own mother now. The terrible experiences he and Alex had been through had made him come to terms with her death and accept that it wasn't his fault! He would never forget her but at last he knew she was no longer waiting to be found amongst the trees.

Blood Brothers

"Why don't you come and see Alex?" asked Jon Barron as he sat in a chair beside Glen's bed in the hospital where they were both being checked over. "Kate's with him. We can all be together."

Neither Jon Barron nor Kate Foster had admonished Glen for what had happened, but they were both obviously deeply traumatised by the boys' two-day disappearance.

Glen looked up at his father and shook his head. "I'm not sure about that."

"He wants to see *you*."

"How can he, after all I put him through?"

"Stop being so defensive," said his father. "OK, you messed up, but you can't go on punishing yourself for ever. Besides, you did really well with the firebreak. You obviously worked together and you both survived, that's what counts."

Then there was a knock at the door and Kate came into the room. She walked straight to Glen's dad's side.

"There's something I – we need to say," she said.

Kate looked tense and nervous and Glen wondered whether she was going to have a real go at him. He waited anxiously.

But instead Kate began, "It may not seem like a very tactful time to bring this up, but your dad asked me to marry him a long time ago – almost as soon as we met. I wanted to, but it didn't seem right when you and Alex hardly knew each other. But now seems the right time to come together as a family." She smiled. "I reckon you two know each other a bit better now."

"We certainly do," said Glen.

"How do you feel about us getting married?" asked his father.

"I feel good," said Glen, surprised at what he was saying, but not feeling in the least threatened by what he'd just heard. "I was a complete idiot. But out there in the wild I began to understand a few things and stopped seeing the world only from my own point of view. Alex and I got to be friends, in the end. But now – I don't know what he'll feel—" Glen's exhaustion returned and he felt weak and apprehensive.

"Alex does want to see you, Glen," said Kate reassuringly. "He really does. He's been able to tell me a bit about what happened. You've been through a terrible experience together and I think you'll find you're pretty close to each other now."

"But you – you must be really angry with me. You must hate me!"

"I don't hate you," said Kate. "I understand how you felt – why you acted as you did. Go and see him. Alex needs you."

"You look lousy," said Glen as he came slowly and hesitantly into Alex's room.

"Thanks."

Glen sat down in a chair by his bedside.

"Don't start all that stuff again," said Alex.

"What stuff?"

"Saying that it was all your fault."

"I *need* to take the blame," Glen half whispered.

"Well, like I said before, don't go on about it!"

There was a long silence, but Glen couldn't detect any hostility. Alex didn't seem to have changed his mind. He and Glen were still friends – really friends.

Then Alex said, "Heard that suggestion – from my mother and your dad?"

"Yes."

"What did you think?"

"What did *you* think?"

Alex suddenly grinned. "I'm not going first."

"Neither am I. At least—" Glen paused. "Actually, I think it's rather a good idea."

"Do you?"

"You're winding me up!"

Alex grinned again. "I've always wanted a brother," he said.

Glen nodded. "So have I, believe it or not. But we're only kind of half brothers, aren't we? Stepbrothers or something?"

Alex shook his head. "I don't think so."

"What are you on about?" asked Glen anxiously.

"We've been through a lot together. After all that, aren't we more like blood brothers?"

"You're right," said Glen. The idea appealed to him very much. "We *are* like blood brothers. I mean – we ended up shedding blood, didn't we?"

"I still can't believe we survived," whispered Alex.

"Do you dream about the bears?" asked Glen. "I'm surprised that I'm not having nightmares!"

"I'm not dreaming about them, but I keep having the same thoughts about them."

"What thoughts?" asked Glen. He was still apprehensive.

"I must be mad after all we went through, but I keep worrying about the mother bear we saw and her cub. Do you think they'll survive?"

"The fire's burnt itself out now and I bet you they survived. The rainy season will be along soon and the forest will begin to grow up again."

"How do you know that?"

"It was on TV."

"I've not been feeling like watching TV," said Alex.

"Well, the bears are back in what's left of the forest, looking for food. I'm sure they'll find some. They're not complete vegetarians, after all!"

"You've made me feel a lot better telling me that," said Alex, leaning back against the pillows.

"Dad and Kate are talking about staying here for a while. They're well behind on the shoot."

"We'll miss out on school," said Alex, and they both laughed as if they had deliberately decided to play truant.

"We learnt more in the wild than we ever would at school," said Glen. "I feel I know myself a bit better now!" he added.

"I know you too," said Alex, and Glen looked at him, worrying yet again. But to his relief Alex was smiling. "Blood brothers," he whispered, his eyes closing. "That's what we are. That's what we'll always be."

If books could kill...

Read about another electrifying encounter with a dangerous predator... the lion!

"Masters knows how to pack a story full of fast-moving incidents, sharply drawn characters and emotional turmoil." *Junior Bookshelf*

ISBN 1 84121 908 8   £4.99

Accident!

Monday, 5pm

The late afternoon heat was still unbearable and to Tom the dusty grasslands seemed endless, an unchanging eternal landscape with the occasional clump of ancient stunted trees. Then, in the distance, he saw foothills, and breathing a sigh of relief returned to the argument he was having with his older brother Josh.

Arno, their guide, was trying not to listen to their quarrelling, keeping his eyes on the uneven track. He was only six years older than Josh, but had become their parents' much-trusted guide during the family's "holiday of a lifetime" in Kenya.

The jeep rocked as Arno attempted to avoid the potholes, while his dog, Ska, a large mongrel who looked like an elongated Alsatian, sat next to Tom in the back, swaying with the movement.

Josh was in the front, hat pulled well down over his eyes, and Tom could see the sweat running down his thick neck. They hadn't been getting on for well over a year now. Tom at thirteen, tall and skinny, had been teasing his brother about carrying too much weight. Josh was fifteen and his face was puffy, lips cracked. His lank, straw-like hair straggled from under his hat, falling damply on to his shoulders.

"You should do some circuit training," said Tom. "Get rid of that paunch."

"It's all muscle," Josh sneered. "*You* look like you've just come out of a refugee camp." Then he paused, remembering that Arno had been a refugee himself, crossing the border into Kenya from Uganda, leaving his family behind, eventually getting work as a guide and 'now knowing the bush better than the locals', as Dad had told them.

"You're so gross." Tom was stung by his brother's insensitivity to Arno's feelings. "What are you? Just so gross."

Always short-tempered, Josh suddenly lost his cool, and bunching his fist he turned and leant over the back of the passenger seat to hit out at his brother.

Tom dodged and Josh punched the air, losing his balance. His whole solid bodyweight lurched into Arno just as the jeep hit a large pothole.

"Get off me!" Arno yelled, grappling for control of the steering. But their guide had hardly got the words out before the jeep veered off the track and skidded sharply into a gully, colliding head-on with the trunk of a tree, then bounced away and rolled over on to its side.

Clouds of choking dust rose and thickened. Slowly, Tom realised he had been thrown out of his seat. He was face-down on the baked, sandy soil, spluttering, eyes smarting.

For a while he lay there, too dazed to move, watching the swirling clouds of dust slowly clear. Then Tom heard a groaning sound and felt a surge of panic. Someone was hurt. Maybe badly. What an irresponsible idiot Josh was!

Tom sat up, mouth as dry as the dust, heart hammering. He couldn't see anything for a moment. Then, with huge relief, he heard Arno's voice.

"Tom, are you all right?" Arno's voice was sharp with anxiety. Short, sturdy and muscular, he radiated authority. But how would he be able to look after them now? thought Tom as he scrambled to his feet and stared at their guide in dismay. Tom and Josh's arguments had caused trouble before – broken windows, hurt feelings, their parents' anger. But this time, they had brought their feud to the wilderness with disastrous results.

"I think so. More than can be said for the jeep," replied Tom.

The vehicle was a shattered wreck, lying on its side with its bonnet stoved in, water streaming from the radiator and a wheel torn off, now some distance away at the back of the gully. Then Tom and Arno heard a groan of pain.

"Where's Josh?" Arno looked frantically around while Ska, who must have leapt clear of the jeep, jumped around them, unhurt.

The low moaning continued.

"Over here!" Arno was already on the other side of the wreck and Tom ran to join him, finding Josh lying on his back, one leg trapped under the overturned vehicle. His face was white, covered in sweat, lips twisted in pain. "We'll have to get the jeep off him," said Arno decisively, muscles bulging as he grabbed the buckled side. "You pull him out." Then seeing Tom's look of despair he added, "He'll be OK. The weight isn't entirely resting on his leg. The jeep's overturned at an angle."

The sweat poured down Arno's brow as he struggled to lift the side of the vehicle, his muscles knotted as he raised the wreckage by at least half a metre.

Amazed by Arno's display of strength, Tom grabbed Josh's shoulders and dragged him away while his brother howled with pain.

"He's clear."

His breath coming in short gasps, Arno let go and the jeep fell back on to its side with a thud.

Tom looked down at his brother's leg which was bent at a strange angle. He felt sick and then *was* sick, turning away from Josh, shoulders heaving, the vomit spreading over the dry grass.

Josh was still moaning in pain as Arno came over and knelt down, checking him out carefully.

"What's hurting?" Tom asked, and then stopped, knowing how stupid he must sound.

"My leg, you idiot!"

"You're lucky," Arno pronounced. "Your leg could easily have been crushed. As it is, I think you've only got a bad break."

"I don't feel lucky," said Josh.

Arno lifted the sleeping bags from the back of the jeep, and Tom helped him to fold them into pillows and unzip one as a cover for Josh. Josh, looking worn out, closed his eyes as if to sleep and Arno and Tom moved a few metres further away.

"What are we going to do?" asked Tom helplessly. "Where *are* we?"

"About nineteen miles from Matendu. It's in the foothills of Mount Elgon," said Arno. "But that's only a small settlement. There's a tribe – the Kala – who live there. But they've deliberately cut themselves off and I don't know what communications they have with the outside world. I don't even know if they've got a radio, but we can try to get in touch with them anyway." Ska was licking at Arno, and then transferred his attentions to Josh, who pushed the dog away.

"What are we going to do if they can't help us?" demanded Tom.

"We'll have to think again," replied Arno enigmatically, increasing Tom's anxiety.

Arno went back to the jeep. He leant cautiously through the broken window, and reached into the front compartment. Not finding what he wanted, he carefully stretched across the steering wheel, pulled out a map from the side pocket, but then continued to search. For the first time since he had met Arno, Tom heard him swear and saw that he was now checking around the outside of the jeep. Arno swore again and held up what was left of the radio. "Like my jeep, it's a write-off. Josh just escaped being crushed, but the radio didn't." He sounded bitter and at a loss.

"Are you insured?" asked Tom. Then he felt ridiculous, as if he was talking about a collision on a safe suburban road. But it was the safe suburban road that he craved. Then a sudden thought came to him and Tom gave a whoop of joy. "I've got a mobile!" He dragged it out of his pocket and began to punch in numbers, but he couldn't get a connection. "Can't be a signal here," he said despondently.

"I thought you'd got a pocket radio." Arno looked hopeful.

"I have, but it's smashed. I must have landed on it."

Arno's face fell and he stared at the horizon. The foothills were bathed in hard-edged sunlight and there was a herd of antelope grazing on the plain, bodies shimmering in the heat. There were zebra too, feeding on the dry grass, as Arno had told them a few minutes before the crash. The temperature was cooler and when Tom glanced down at his watch he saw it was now just before seven pm.

"What are we going to do?" Tom asked again.

"Camp here for the night. What else *can* we do? If only you guys had some control this wouldn't have happened." Arno sounded contemptuous. Tom felt angry. Josh was the one who'd been behaving like a kid, and had put them all at risk, not him.

Then, very suddenly, the sun went down. There was no twilight; it was as if a dark blanket had been thrown over the light.

"Why does the sun go down so fast?" asked Tom. He'd noticed the phenomenon before, but hadn't been curious enough to ask. Now, out here on the plain, the sun's sudden departure was much more obvious.

"It's because we're on the Equator," replied Arno. "The sun goes down at seven pm all the year round."

Snapped into darkness, Tom felt a wave of fear which he tried to control.

"Let's take a look at Josh," said Arno.

He appeared to be sleeping. Tom and Arno stood over him. Arno was looking at him carefully, apparently satisfied.

"Should he be asleep?" asked Tom.

"Yes – the pain will have exhausted him. He'll be fine."

"You're sure?"

"I'm not sure about anything," snapped Arno. "But I'll make Josh as comfortable as I can and in the morning I'll hike to Matendu. I hope to God the Kala *have* got a radio because, if not—" Arno paused.

"If not?" prompted Tom, the anxiety rising from the pit of his stomach.

"I'll have to try to reach Osak." He picked up the map and studied it carefully. "They've got a landing strip, but it's a long way away from here. Thirty miles. Maybe more."

Tom felt an overwhelming sense of inadequacy and a creeping fear. This was the African grasslands – lion country. Before the accident they had been hoping to spot a pride from the safety of the jeep. But now the jeep wasn't safe any longer and neither were they.

During their visit to Kenya, Tom, Josh and their parents, Alan and Liz Trent, had already seen elephants, buffalo, monkeys and other wild animals, but they hadn't as yet sighted lion. Then, just as they were about to go on the best trip of the holiday, a five-day tour 'lion hunting' including two days' camping at the end, Dad had picked up a tummy bug and Mum had elected to stay with him in the hotel.

"You go with Arno," Dad had said. "You can't come to Africa without seeing a lion. Arno's absolutely reliable and, who knows, you might get a lion in your lens." Dad had been talking about Josh's new video camera which was now somewhere in the wreck of the jeep – presumably smashed like the radios.

Tom turned to Arno who was still bending over the map.

"I'm sorry," said Tom.

"Mmm?" Arno was engrossed.

"The crash was our fault. Josh's always determined to have an argument. But this was one too many." Tom paused and then asked, "Why can't we make it to the Kala at Matendu tonight?"

Arno sighed and then made eye contact with Tom for the first time since the crash. He spoke slowly and patiently. "Because it's too dangerous to wander about after dark. I've told you about all the wild animals we could encounter already. So we're stranded until tomorrow morning. When we don't arrive at Kisimu on Wednesday evening, your parents will report us missing and the helicopter will come looking for us. I'll try the Kala before then in any case." Arno called to Ska, who came loping across obediently. But Tom thought he could see fear in the dog's eyes. Arno stroked Ska affectionately and then went back to the jeep again. "I'll try and get him a bowl of water."

Tom suddenly realised how thirsty *he* was – and what about Josh? Then he heard Arno give a muffled cry and

Tom could hardly bring himself to ask what was wrong.

"What's up now?"

"The water canisters have got punctured." For the first time there was real anxiety in Arno's voice.

"No water?"

"Not a drop."

"What about the bottles?"

"There's a small amount left in each. Don't you remember me saying we'd need to stop soon and fill them up from the canisters?"

Tom did, but he'd been quarrelling with Josh at the time. He looked down at his brother's pale, sweaty face and suddenly remembered him as a shy child whom he'd once wanted to protect – even though Josh was his big brother. Why had he forgotten that now they were older? Despite the fact that they were opposites, they had got on well together until the last couple of years. Suddenly Josh opened his eyes.

"How do you feel?"

"Terrible." Every time he tried to move Josh winced with pain. "Any water?" Clearly he'd not heard the bad news.

Tom hesitated and Arno came across, kneeling

down by Josh's side.

"We have a water problem," he said gently.

"But there are two canisters."

"Didn't you hear what I said to Tom? They're punctured."

Josh closed his eyes against the grim reality of their plight. "I was asleep," he murmured. He looked as if he'd fall asleep again any moment.

Arno spoke again. "We've got some left in the water bottles, but that's only a little. We need to conserve what we have."

Tom glanced at Arno pleadingly. "Isn't there any water round here at all?"

Arno was studying the map again. "There's a waterhole about three miles away. Could be a little further."

"I thought you knew the area so well." Tom wanted to shift the blame. Wasn't Arno meant to be their guide?

Arno didn't reply and there was a long silence, broken by Josh groaning.

Wanting to walk away from the situation, Tom climbed up to the top of the gully and looked out across the plain, which was vast and featureless. In the darkness nothing was distinct and the grassland looked more like a huge lake, making him even more thirsty. Their predicament was appalling, he thought. However would they survive without water, let alone get back to civilisation and medical help for Josh? Then he realised that being alone with his own thoughts was much worse than being with the others. After all, Arno was in charge. Surely it was his responsibility to get them out of trouble! Of course he'd get them out of trouble. He was a professional guide, hired to show them the sights and look after them if they got into danger. Wasn't he?

Tom scrambled back into the gully, still conscious that he and Josh had always regarded Arno as the ultimate super-guide with everything at his fingertips. But at the moment he seemed to have alarmingly little to contribute.

"I've got a first-aid kit, but it's only designed for minor injuries. Your brother needs to have his leg set. Maybe I can rig up a splint."

Arno was talking as if Josh wasn't there. Who is this

guy anyway? wondered Tom. We don't know anything about him. His fear increased again, turning into a kind of dread at being stranded in this wilderness with a stranger.

"What about that helicopter?" Tom asked tentatively.

"It should come looking eventually, but not for days yet. We've already talked about this."

"*Should?*"

"One of the choppers is being overhauled and that puts a lot of strain on the rescue service. There *is* another aircraft, but it could be out on some other emergency. And with them not expecting us at Kisimu until Wednesday evening..."

"So what are we going to do till then?" Tom questioned aggressively.

"I've got some painkillers and I can give Josh one of those, which will help." There was a brief pause. "We'd be stupid to try and carry him to Matendu between us, even in the morning. Don't forget, this is lion territory. At least I've got a gun, and it's still working – despite the accident. In fact, the gun's about the only thing that *is* working. We have to be careful."

You have to be careful, thought Tom, defensively. It's *your* job to be careful, not ours.

Ska began to bark and Josh's groaning intensified. As a result, Arno seemed even more anxious. He went to fetch the water bottles from the jeep. Three out of the four of them were empty. Arno stared at them thoughtfully, then put them into a shoulder bag.

"Maybe I *should* try and make the waterhole. There's a chance it could be dry, though."

"But you said we shouldn't wander about in lion country," snapped Tom. Make up your mind, he thought savagely. You should be our leader. Not that you're much good at it.

"We don't have much choice, do we? We need water. We're going to have to take a risk."

"Look," said Tom. "Why can't I go for the water?"

"Don't be stupid."

"I'm not." Tom was resentful. "I've done a lot of orienteering at school – as a team sport. I'm good."

"But not good enough for out here."

"What do you mean?"

"This is Africa."

"So?"

"It's the wild."

"Well – are you going to go?"

Arno shook his head. "Not tonight. I should stay with Josh. He needs a splint for that leg and I must put up a tent and rig up a mosquito net for him. Well – for all of us."

"So I'll go for the water."

"Not now. We must wait until morning," said Arno.

"I can't do that." Suddenly Tom realised how incredibly thirsty he was. And there was something else in the back of his mind. He needed to prove himself to Arno after messing up in the jeep. Tom remembered how many times he had done this at school and at home. The climb up the cliff face, the running in the rain, riding a moto-cross bike when he had no experience, the jump across the ditches on the marsh. Why had he done all these things? Maybe to put himself in first place? He didn't know. Maybe to put Josh in *his* place. Second place. But now he had to care for Josh. He had broken his leg and would wake up even more thirsty in the morning. Tom wanted to get water for him, and he wasn't going to listen to their guide – the hired hand. He should be the one to help

Josh, not a stranger, paid for by Dad.

"You'll have to wait," said Arno firmly.

"How would *you* get to that waterhole, anyway?" Tom asked casually.

"I'd use a compass and the map," said Arno, relieved that Tom wasn't challenging him any more. Holding out the map, he showed Tom the compass direction he would follow – north-west all the way.

Arno was in 'guide' mode again – relaxed, in charge. Suddenly, acting on impulse, Tom grabbed the map, compass and shoulder bag containing the water bottles from their surprised guide and ran away from the camp, as quickly as ever he'd run in any race.

Arno was furious, shaking his fist and calling out to Tom. "Come back!" he shouted. "Come back *now*."

But Tom ran on, oblivious to his entreaties. He knew Arno wouldn't come after him. He couldn't leave Josh. Soon Arno was only a tiny, indignant figure in the distance.

How on earth would he manage, Tom suddenly wondered, now that he had got his own way. Water? Lions? Living in Ealing hadn't exactly equipped him for survival in a wilderness and he found himself longing for the quiet routine of school and home. But then he recalled how good he was at running and felt an unexpected rush of confidence. Orienteering – finding the route and running through difficult terrain – was his greatest talent, and with his long thin frame Tom was built for long-distance running. Even Josh had to admit that. He'd managed to get away from Arno. But would his running skills help him to the waterhole now?

Suddenly Tom began to panic, sure he'd been a complete fool to run off like this, defying Arno and putting himself at incredible risk. But he *had* to get water. He couldn't possibly last the night without drinking – or so he thought. And he was sure Josh couldn't either. As a result, he'd had to take the law into his own hands. But what had he done?

All too quickly, Tom realised he'd plunged himself into the African bush – a highly dangerous environment which should have been viewed from a vehicle rather than penetrated on foot. Tom paused, listening. It seemed he was surrounded by danger – danger that he had no idea how to cope with.

Thirst

Tom looked out at the darkening plain. It was amazing how safe the jeep had made him feel. Now the vehicle was wrecked, he could no longer be driven through the wilderness. Instead he was on his feet and alone.

Despite the cooling night air, sweat was glistening on Tom's brow as he jogged on. Each bottle would hold about a litre. There was a tiny bit of precious water slopping about in the bottom of each of them. Tom was already incredibly thirsty and was sure he could drink the lot at one go. Then he realised that if he did find water he could fill a bottle and drink as much as he liked – as long as he put iodine tablets in it first. He could fill all the bottles after that. Cheered by the thought, Tom began to run faster, the ground dry and dusty beneath his feet, the full moon giving the grasslands a strange, silvery sheen.

Fortunately there was still a track, maybe the same one that Arno had been going to follow in the jeep, and this at least was reassuring. Tom glanced back and could just make out Arno and Ska sitting a little distance from the jeep, far away. He didn't think Arno could see him, though. Just as well.

As he ran on, Tom began to realise how out of shape he had become. The three-week holiday that Dad had saved up for for so long hadn't exactly been physically demanding. They had sat on planes and in buses and taxis for what seemed like a very long time, and then, for the last three days, in Arno's jeep. At first Tom had found this frustrating, limiting his appreciation of what they were seeing, but gradually he had grown used to it and to love Kenya. The plain in particular held a magical quality, with stunning beauty and rare animals and a sense of eternity.

Tom kept checking the compass. So far he seemed to be on the right bearing, but he hadn't been running for long and already he was beginning to gasp for breath, his throat as dry as the arid landscape. He was wearing shorts and a T-shirt and a pair of old trainers. They were comfortable, but he wondered if they were going to stand the pressure of the run. A few trees were beginning to appear more frequently now, but they were shrivelled, barely alive, and boulders rose menacingly on either side. He could hear the sound of crickets and they made him feel wary and uneasy.

Tom had always been confident at both schoolwork and sport, and he'd always got on well with his parents. So why did Josh irritate him so much? he wondered. But he knew the answer all too well. For some reason his parents always seemed to cosset Josh, to protect him, while Tom was left to make his own way. Why was Josh such a favourite? He had once asked his father the burning question and had been told, "We don't have a favourite. But Josh finds life a bit more of a struggle, son. Not like you. He needs support." Why should Josh get all the help? Tom had wondered at the time, and still did.

But now their rivalry had plunged them all into disaster and he felt bitterly ashamed of himself for the first time.

Tom was now approaching the foothills and his heart was thumping painfully as he prayed that the waterhole wasn't dry. The promise of water was now becoming an obsession and Tom saw himself lying on his stomach by the side of the waterhole, lapping like a dog.

Again his thoughts turned to Arno. Who *was* Arno? He and Josh were in a serious situation, totally dependent on someone who might turn out to be more unpredictable than they could have anticipated. And here he was, looking for water, leaving his injured brother in the hands of a stranger.

Panic gripped him and Tom had to force himself to calm down. It was natural to him to take the lead – he had no problem with that – and he was reasonably self-reliant. But this unfamiliar, dangerous setting was making him feel distinctly out of his depth. Though Josh was even more so, he thought to himself.

Josh was a couch potato, lying on the sofa, watching as many videos and playing as many games as he could pack into a week. He, Tom, was a highly motivated student, heading for university. Josh was lazy and switched-off, doing as little work as he could get away with, and regularly truanting. While Josh was shy and introverted, practically friendless, Tom was the opposite, with a wide social circle because he had such an outgoing personality.

So was Josh a rebel or just a dropout? Tom didn't know, but what he did know was that Josh hadn't always been like this. At eleven, his brother had been quite fit and athletic, a keen footballer and doing OK at school. So what had gone wrong?

Tom ran on, mouth dry but his speed gradually improving, somehow slipping into the rhythm of his running, drawing on his energy reserves.

Tom checked the compass again and saw that he was still on the right bearing. He must have already covered a couple of kilometres, so where was this water? Tom began to fantasise, seeing a crystal-clear lake with clean, cold water rippled by a darting breeze, but the foothills were as gaunt and arid as the plain, the sandy surface littered with boulders.

In a lapse of concentration, Tom stumbled as the slope rose again, but as he took up the rhythm of his running he imagined he could at last see water, glinting in the moonlight, beckoning him on.

Tom began to gasp for breath again, his legs feeling like lead, his thirst almost overcoming him as he reached a large dip in the ground and came to a stumbling halt. Clouds were scudding across the moon and he couldn't see anything properly in the relative darkness, but Tom was sure he could hear a soft, lapping sound.

Joyfully he began to move towards the depression in the ground, which was suddenly illuminated by moonlight. But Tom couldn't see any water and his joy turned to despair. This couldn't be the place. The small depression might once have been some kind of shallow dew pond, but now there was nothing but dust.

PREDATOR

Can you combat Lion Country?

Read the rest of *Killer Instinct* to find out what happens next!

Are you ready to face White Death?

**A fin zigzags through the water.
Jack knows it's a shark attack.**

Someone's going to get eaten alive. But there's
one fatal difference. This is no movie. No video
game. It's all for real – and Jack's the victim…

ISBN 1 84121 906 1   £4.99

Will you outrun the Wolf Pack?

A hungry wolf waits for the thrill of the kill. Luke knows the score.
Soon the hunted will be a blood trail. It could be cool TV. But this isn't a survival game show. It's all happening in real time. And Luke's playing for the big prize – his life.

ANTHONY MASTERS

ISBN 1 84121 904 5   £4.99

More Orchard Red Apples

Predator

❏ Shark Attack	Anthony Masters	1 84121 906 1	£4.99
❏ Hunted	Anthony Masters	1 84121 904 5	£4.99
❏ Killer Instinct	Anthony Masters	1 84121 908 8	£4.99

Danger

❏ Aftershock!	Tony Bradman	1 84121 552 X	£3.99
❏ Hurricane!	Tony Bradman	1 84121 588 0	£3.99

Jiggy McCue Stories

❏ The Poltergoose	Michael Lawrence	1 86039 836 7	£4.99
❏ The Killer Underpants	Michael Lawrence	1 84121 713 1	£4.99
❏ The Toilet of Doom	Michael Lawrence	1 84121 752 2	£4.99
❏ Maggot Pie	Michael Lawrence	1 84121 756 5	£4.99
❏ The Fire Within	Chris d'Lacey	1 84121 533 3	£4.99
❏ The Salt Pirates of Skegness	Chris d'Lacey	1 84121 539 2	£4.99

Orchard Red Apples are available from all good bookshops,
or can be ordered direct from the publisher:
Orchard Books, PO BOX 29, Douglas IM99 1BQ
Credit card orders please telephone 01624 836000 or fax 01624 837033
or e-mail: bookshop@enterprise.net for details.

To order please quote title, author and ISBN
and your full name and address.
Cheques and postal orders should be made payable to"Bookpost plc.'
Postage and packing is FREE within the UK
(overseas customers should add £1.00 per book).

Prices and availability are subject to change